I'm not even halfway through my first packet of cheese 'n' onion when the door opens and standing there is Nicola Cohen.

'Hi, Mickey,' she says, shutting the door behind her.

She's got some nerve, I'll give her that.

'How did you find me?' I ask.

'I'm an investigative journalist, Mickey. We find things out.'

'Yeah,' I say. 'Well, detectives find things out too.'

Reviews of Mickey's other cases, *Sharp Stuff* and *Sharp Shot*:

'A smart debut, packed with funny lines' *Observer*

'Lively and funny with an all-too-sharp picture of school life'   *Children's Book News*

'Let's not beat about the bush: this is a gem ... The second Mickey Sharp case crackles with wit, invention and insight' *School Librarian*

'Stuffed full of hilarious characters, top teen observations and jokes ... Dominic Barker has played a blinder!'   *The Times*

Also available by Dominic Barker:

Sharp Stuff
Sharp Shot

A MICKEY SHARP CASE

SHARP RETURNS

SHARP RETURNS
A CORGI BOOK : 0552 54843X

Published in Great Britain by Corgi Books,
an imprint of Random House Children's Books

This edition published 2003

1 3 5 7 9 10 8 6 4 2

Papers used by Random House Children's Books are natural,
recyclable products made from wood grown in sustainable forests.
The manufacturing processes conform to the environmental
regulations of the country of origin.

Set in 12/14 pt Palatino by
Falcon Oast Graphic Art Ltd.

Corgi Books are published by Random House Children's Books,
61–63 Uxbridge Road, London W5 5SA,
a division of The Random House Group Ltd,
in Australia by Random House Australia (Pty) Ltd,
20 Alfred Street, Milsons Point, Sydney, NSW 2061, Australia,
in New Zealand by Random House New Zealand Ltd,
18 Poland Road, Glenfield, Auckland 10, New Zealand,
and in South Africa by Random House (Pty) Ltd,
Endulini, 5A Jubilee Road, Parktown 2193, South Africa

THE RANDOM HOUSE GROUP Limited Reg. No. 954009
www.kidsatrandomhouse.co.uk

A CIP catalogue record for this book is available from the British
Library.

Printed and bound in Great Britain by
Bookmarque Ltd, Croydon, Surrey

A MICKEY SHARP CASE
SHARP RETURNS

DOMINIC BARKER

CORGI BOOKS

To Mary, my gran

The author gratefully acknowledges the assistance of Michael Barker and the K. Blundell Trust.

CHAPTER 1

You stare at a door long enough and it's got to open eventually. I mean, if it doesn't it might as well be a wall, right? Someone puts a handle and hinges on a piece of wood and gives you a guarantee. They're saying that sooner or later someone is going to turn the handle, give the door a push and walk in. Aren't they? Otherwise what's the point in having a door in the first place? It might as well be a . . . I'm going round in circles.

I'm going round in circles because I'm waiting. It's the hardest thing about being a detective. Not the waiting when you're on a case. That's boring, but at least you're waiting for something definite. But waiting for a case is worse because there mightn't be anybody out there who's ever going to give you one. You might be like those Japanese soldiers they dropped on tiny islands in some war that Mr Kemp was going on about in History. They dumped one soldier on each island to defend it against the Americans. It seems a dumb thing to do to me – drop one soldier on an island and expect him to defend it on his own – but that's what they did. And then when the war was over they forgot about them and thirty years later they found one by accident and he was still guarding the island and waiting to kill the Americans while all the other Japanese were now best friends with the Americans and selling them cheap cameras.

It's all my family's fault. They won't let me put our phone number in my advert in the paper because my sister says she'll get phone calls from perverts and weirdos. I don't understand what she's worried about because most of her friends are perverts and weirdos. But my mum and dad said no as well because they don't want to get phone calls from people trying to sell them things, even though the people trying to sell things haven't got a hope because my family hasn't got any money because my dad can't get a job. They make him go to the Job Centre now to learn about computers and how to write a letter because of something called the New Deal. It seems stupid to me. My dad doesn't want to know how to use a computer and he already knows how to write a letter but they make him go anyway. He gets into a really bad mood and shouts at me as soon as he gets home. It might be a New Deal for him but it's a lousy deal for me.

I suggested we had a second line installed in the shed where my office is, but they wouldn't go with that either. 'We haven't got enough money to waste on your stupid detective nonsense,' and all that stuff that parents do so well. And my sister went mad and said that if anyone should have an extra line it should be her because she's older and has 'issues that need to be discussed in private', which means talking to her mates about boys or diets or which bit of their bodies to get pierced next. Some of her friends have got so much metal in them they could be recycled.

I pull open the top drawer of my desk and drag out a Coke and a packet of crisps. It's my fifth Coke today and my fourth packet of crisps. When you're bored your consumption goes up. I lean back, put my feet up and twist the top off the Coke. This is a big mistake because it explodes. I don't know what it is with Coke. Some of the bottles explode and some of them don't. I reckon there must be some guy in the Coke factory who really hates his job and he shakes one bottle in ten really hard. And they're the ones that explode all over you. Normally you have a chance to get out of the way, but not if you've got your feet up on a desk. It all spills into my lap.

Now the thing with Coke is that it's OK to drink but when it splashes all over you it's not the most comfortable feeling. I get over to the corner where I chucked a cloth I used to clean up the shed a few weeks ago. It's a bit mucky but it might soak up some of the stuff. I start wiping down my jeans. Which is precisely when the door opens and a boy walks in.

'Oh,' he says. He's not impressed.

'I had an accident,' I tell him.

I realize that I sound like I've just wet myself. 'With a bottle of Coke,' I tell him. 'That bottle of Coke.'

He looks at the bottle of Coke and then he looks at me. 'Mmm,' he says.

'What do you want?' I ask.

'I'm looking for the detective,' he says.

'You've found him.'

'Oh. Look, maybe this isn't a good time.'

'Yes it is,' I tell him.

'I could come back when you're drier.'

'No need,' I tell him. 'Sit down.' I indicate a box as I've only got one chair.

'Perhaps it's not really that important.'

'Sure it is. Sit down.'

'Well . . .'

'Come on.'

I've had some awkward clients already but I've never had one I had to beg to sit down.

'You're sure it's all right?'

'Yes.'

I want to pick him up and chuck him onto the box. Only that probably wouldn't be the best way to turn him into a paying customer.

He looks at the box. Then he wipes it with his hand. Then he apologizes for wiping it with his hand. Then he gives it another good look and then finally he sits down on it.

'So, what's the case?' I say.

'I don't know.' He starts looking round again. 'Perhaps this is all going too far. I could be imagining things.'

'Look,' I say. 'You might be imagining things or you might not so I'm the guy you need to find out. I'm experienced in this type of thing.' I can't resist a line like this but it gets me into trouble.

'Oh, you're experienced, are you?' he says brightly. 'Have you got any references?'

11

'What?' I say. I think I know what he means but I'm not sure.

'Testimonials from satisfied customers. Reports saying what a good job you did. I'd like to see them.'

There's a problem there. I've had two clients. One of them hasn't spoken to me since I solved her case and the other one moved to Los Angeles. I can't see either of them giving me a reference.

'Listen,' I say. 'In my business people aren't too willing to put their signatures to documents, if you know what I mean.'

I'm rather pleased with that. It makes me sound tough. I take a swig of Coke to add to the effect but I do it a bit too fast and all the bubbles shoot up my nose and I end up coughing, with bits of Coke dribbling out, which kind of spoils the effect.

'I suppose I can see your point,' he says. 'Let me just marshal my thoughts so I can put the problem concisely.'

I don't know exactly what he means but I get the idea that he's going to tell me what's on his mind so I keep my mouth shut until he's ready. Then I remember that this would be a good time to commit his appearance and behaviour to memory. Detectives should always do that and I keep forgetting.

He doesn't seem to have any facial tics or twitches which is a bit disappointing. I always look out for facial tics because they almost always mean that someone can't be trusted but I've only ever seen one and that was on our music teacher on Friday afternoon when the morons at the back got hold of the bongos.

There's something about this kid, though. He's too neat. His hair's all straight and parted on one side and his blazer looks like it would on a Year Seven on his first day at school and his tie's the right length. His face is kind of thin and he's got no spots or anything. He looks just like my mum would want me to look in my school uniform.

And then I realize the weird thing about him. He's still wearing school uniform. I mean, it's my school's uniform, which is why I didn't particularly notice it before, but it's almost two hours since school finished. Now one thing I know about all normal kids is that they get their school uniform off the moment they get home. School uniforms are all ugly. They're definite proof that adults hate children. They can wear whatever they want but they get to tell us what to wear. The sociology teacher at our school, Mr Jarvis, wears T-shirts, jeans and trainers but nobody sends him home with a letter from the Head.

All I know is this: there's something wrong with you if you wear a school uniform when you don't have to.

'It's the election,' he says suddenly out of nothing.

'What election?' I ask.

He looks surprised. 'You go to Hanford High, don't you?'

'Yeah.'

'Well, the election there, you know?'

I shake my head.

'Don't you listen in assembly?'

Now there's one dumb question. I didn't think anybody listened in assembly. There's no point. All assemblies are exactly the same. Don't drop litter. Don't run in the corridor. Don't fight. Don't throw doughnuts at the canteen staff. Well, the last one might just be my school but everything else is exactly the same. Once you've heard one assembly you've heard them all. Why waste your life listening to the same things over and over again?

'The assembly about being Head Boy,' he reminds me.

And then it comes back to me. I had listened to an assembly after all. I just hope nobody ever finds out. That kind of information can ruin your credibility.

Walton, that's the Head of our school, had come in and said that as part of the government's new citizenship initiative or something we were going to have our first taste of democracy. Democracy means everyone gets a say in what happens. Walton made it sound like poison. He said this year we were going to be able to vote for Head Boy and Head Girl. Normally he picks them and he always picks the kind of kids that make you want to be sick. The only marks they've ever got in their lives are As and their parents are always governors. They're supposed to be role models or something and you're supposed to look up to them. But nobody does. Everybody thinks they must be the biggest crawlers in the world. The way to get respect in my school is to win fights, smoke cigarettes and be able to drink four cans of lager without throwing up. I'm not saying it's right but it's the way it is.

Anyway, Walton made this big deal of how he was trusting us and how he didn't want us to let him down. I don't know why he bothers saying things like that. We always let him down and he knows we're going to. It's the deal between teachers and kids.

And then he started on about litter and a member of the canteen staff having to go to hospital after being hit by a doughnut and I stopped listening. If they didn't make the doughnuts so hard then they wouldn't be that dangerous.

'There's no point beating about the bush,' the kid announces suddenly. 'I want to be Head Boy.'

I always knew that being a detective might be tough but I never realized that it was going to be as bad as this. Working for the Head Boy. If that gets out, my reputation is shot.

But I'm a detective. And a desperate detective at that. I've got to take the cases that come.

'OK,' I say. 'But I thought you had to be in Year Eleven.'

'I *am* in Year Eleven,' he says, a bit annoyed.

'Just checking,' I say to cover up the fact that I thought he was in Year Eight. He's small. 'So what's that got to do with me?'

'The election is next week,' he tells me,

'and strange things have been happening. I put some posters up and they all got ripped down.'

'People are always ripping things down,' I tell him. They only bother having wall displays in our school when the inspectors come.

'And other things,' he says. 'My friends have stopped talking to me.'

That's hardly surprising either. I'd stop talking to somebody who made a fool of himself by going round saying he wanted to be Head Boy.

'And,' he says, letting his voice drop to a whisper, 'I got a C in History.'

'What's weird about that?' I ask. 'I've got Cs in History too when I've been trying.'

'No,' he insists, 'you don't understand. I've never got anything less than an A in my whole life.'

What did I tell you?

'So, you did a bad piece of work.'

'No.' He shakes his head. 'My analysis of the relationship between Mary Queen of Scots and Elizabeth I was knowledgeable, insightful and readable.'

'You sure?' I say, not really being qualified to comment on the subject myself.

'Absolutely. There's something fishy going on.'

It doesn't sound like that to me. It all sounds perfectly explicable. His posters were torn down like everything else, his mates are embarrassed by him wanting to be Head Boy and the teacher had an off night. Teachers do, you know. You see them marking stuff in cover lessons. They don't read it. They just tick it and then write down a letter depending on how neat your handwriting looks. Trust me.

Still, it's not my job to go round talking my clients out of cases just because I happen to think they're being paranoid. It's my job to keep the client happy and take the money. Which brings me to the thing I always find the most difficult.

'I charge six pounds a day plus expenses.' I decide to have a go at putting my prices up. You don't get anywhere if you don't try.

'Fine,' he says.

I feel great. He didn't even try to beat me down. Then I feel stupid. Why didn't I ask for ten?

'I'll need a couple of posters,' I say.

'OK,' he says. 'I'll meet you before school tomorrow, outside the main gate, and give you some.' He stands up to go.

'One more thing,' I say. I know I shouldn't ask but I can't resist. 'Why do you want to be Head Boy? Is it just a show-off thing?'

He looks at me like he's really offended and for a second I think he's going to take the case back off me and walk out, which would serve me right for opening my big mouth when I should have kept it shut.

'A show-off thing?' he says indignantly. 'You think that I'm someone who wants a meaningless title like Head Boy merely to feed my own ego? You think it would have crossed my mind to be Head Boy if it were in the gift of Mr Walton? Think no such thing. I want to change the school for the better and to give us a say in our own education. With an overwhelming mandate from the pupils I'll have the power to go to Mr Walton and demand real changes.'

I haven't understood everything he said but I think I've got the general idea.

'What changes?'

'I've got to go,' he tells me. 'Read this.' He pulls a leaflet out of his pocket and bangs it down on my desk. 'See you tomorrow morning,' he adds. 'Don't be late.'

And then he walks out.

I pick up the leaflet. It says:

VOTE FOR CARL MARKS
AND YOU'LL BE VOTING FOR

1) Voluntary school uniform
2) A homework cap (no more than thirty minutes a night)
3) Select your own teachers
4) Individual shower cubicles in the PE block

Well, if nothing else, he's got my vote.

CHAPTER 2

'And now for the bulletin.'

It's the next morning and I'm sitting in my form room watching Mr Newman, my form teacher, battle through registration. Everybody starts talking as soon as he says it's the bulletin. The bulletin is this piece of paper that says what's going on in school that day. Nobody cares and it's always the same so they don't listen.

Through the noise I can hear odd bits.

'Lost property . . . music lessons . . . Year Nine hockey team disqualified from inter-school cup for assaulting referee . . . doughnuts no longer to be sold in the school canteen . . . hustings for Head Boy and Girl to be held . . . Year Nine parents' evening . . . pupil who keeps ringing up Pizza Paradise and getting Double Deluxe with Salami, Cheese and Extra Gherkins delivered to Mr Walton's home address has been permanently excluded . . . That's it.'

There are some times when being a

detective is a hard job. This is one of those times. I put my hand up.

'Yes, Mickey.'

'Could you read the bulletin again, sir?'

All the talking in the class just stops. It's amazing how kids can all be talking but somehow they hear right away when someone says something a bit strange.

Newman looks at me weirdly. 'I beg your pardon, Mickey.'

'Could you ... er ... read the bulletin again?'

The class stay silent. Newman keeps looking at me. 'Is this some kind of joke?'

This is typical. Show a bit of interest in something and teachers automatically think that you're trying to mess them around. That kind of sums our school up.

'No,' I say. 'I just want to hear the bulletin again.'

The class is still too amazed to speak. Nobody has ever wanted to hear the bulletin again.

'Why didn't you listen the first time?' demands Newman suspiciously. You can see that he still thinks I'm trying to wind him up.

'I was listening but I didn't hear one bit.'

'Which bit?'

I'm trapped now. 'The ... er ... bit about the Head Boy.'

The class erupts into laughter. I feel myself starting to go red.

'Mickey wants to be Head Boy,' yells a moron at the back.

'He's not even a Boy,' shouts another.

'He's a girl,' says the third.

'He's gay,' they all shout together.

The morons at the back love calling people gay. It's their favourite insult at the moment and they use it all the time. If some boy has a new haircut, he's gay. If some boy answers a question in class, he's gay. If some boy doesn't want to have a fight, he's gay, and if some boy touches another boy by accident he's double, triple, quadruple gay. I don't think they even know what being gay is. But it doesn't stop them shouting. And sometimes, even though you know they're morons, it doesn't make it any easier.

Newman shuts them up after a bit and then turns back to me. 'You really want me to read it again?' He still doesn't believe me.

I nod.

'All right,' he says, looking confused. 'But if people are going to start showing interest in the bulletin then we're going to have to reassess the whole way we do registration.'

He pauses. I think he thinks he's just made a joke. Nobody laughs though. Teachers are never funny when they try to be. It's embarrassing watching them.

He coughs and then reads the bit out: 'Hustings are to be held for the new Head Boy and Head Girl at lunch time in the sports hall. Everybody in the school is welcome to attend.'

I don't want to but I know I've got to ask another question. 'What's hustings?'

Lots of sucking noises from the morons at the back. You can see why nobody learns anything in our school. Every time anybody asks a question they get insulted.

'Are you on drugs, Mickey?' asks Newman. Another pause. Another silence. Another teacher attempt at humour goes down the toilet.

He coughs again. 'Hustings are a meeting where the candidates for a particular job all say why they want it and why they'd be good at it and then they can be asked questions. The idea is to give the electorate an informed choice about who to vote for. So at lunch time anybody who wants to be Head Boy or Girl will speak and you can decide which of them you think will do the best job.'

The class start talking again about two seconds into his answer but I heard enough to understand. That's my lunch time taken care of then. I'll have to see what Carl Marks's opposition is like.

The classroom door opens and Katie Pierce and Julie Reece walk in. Late as always. They walk straight past Newman without even acknowledging his existence like they always do.

Newman's lips tighten up. 'Late detention for you two,' he says.

'Had to see Mr Walton,' shouts back Katie without bothering to turn round.

'Got a note?' says Newman.

'No,' says Katie. 'Go and ask him.'

'If you're late for school without a note explaining why, then you're automatically in late detention.'

'Mr Walton said we didn't need one,' snaps back Katie. 'So, we won't go. Put us in if you want but I don't think Mr Walton will be very pleased when we go and see him about it. We might be very upset and cry about how horrible you've been to us, when we came into school especially early today.'

'Yeah,' says Julie. 'My hair was still wet.'

You can tell by Newman's face that he wishes he'd never got into this. Katie Pierce is Walton's little pet because her mum's a school governor and so whenever she gets into trouble she just tells him, pretends to cry and he gets her out of it. She treats all the teachers like they're dirt and nothing ever happens to her.

Newman's trying to work out whether she's lying. It's tough with Katie Pierce because she's good. I've been watching her lie for three years and I'm still not sure. But I figure that the Walton thing is probably the truth because you can check it out too easily. If you've got a choice of lies to tell a teacher, pick the one that's going to be hardest to track down. Most of them say they'll check your story out but in the end they can't be bothered. They'd rather just rush off home as soon as the bell goes. They had to put speed bumps in the road out of the school car park to stop them driving away so fast.

After a bit Newman starts off on this lecture about how he expects pupils to show courtesy, to stop when they enter the classroom and explain where they've been, but he doesn't fill in a late slip. Katie's won and everybody knows it.

And then right in the middle of his lecture a phone starts ringing. Katie sticks her hand in her bag and pulls her phone out.

'I'm talking to you,' says Newman.

Katie flips open her phone and says, 'Hello.'

Newman starts walking towards her. His face is going red. 'Don't answer the phone when I'm talking,' he shouts.

Katie says something else.

'I said don't talk to someone else while I'm talking to you.'

Katie keeps talking.

'Give me that phone.'

Newman's right by her desk now. You can see that he'd like to grab it off her. But he can't. If he touched her, her mother would get him sacked.

'Later,' says Katie and flips down the top.

'Give me that phone,' Newman holds his hand out.

'I can't do that, I'm afraid,' says Katie in a really calm voice. 'My mother says I must keep my phone at all times in case of emergencies.'

'You're in a classroom,' Newman yells at

her. 'In a school. That's not a place for chatting to your friends.'

Newman's fooling himself there. Classrooms are exactly the place for chatting to your friends.

'How was I to know it wasn't an emergency?' asks Katie.

Newman swallows hard. He can't think of an answer to that one. 'When you found out it was one of your friends you should have hung up,' he says. But you can see he's losing.

'Oh I couldn't do that, sir,' Katie tells him. 'That would have been rude.'

And then the bell goes.

Katie picks up her bag and walks round Newman towards the door. The rest of the class do the same. Newman just stands in the same place. Something in the side of his face starts twitching. I figure he must be contemplating a crime.

CHAPTER 3

I didn't get a chance to look at the corridor walls before registration because I was a bit late and I didn't want to get stuck with detention. But I'm in no hurry to get to French and so I take my time and check them out. Normally our school walls are not the most interesting things to look at. Just bits of graffiti and torn pieces of faded work by kids who you know are in Year Ten but have got Year Seven by their names. But things are different today.

The walls are plastered with posters. They weren't there at the end of school yesterday – even I would have noticed. They're weird. Most of the poster is dominated by this black silhouette of a boy's head and then underneath it says,

VOTE LEJEUNE
BE COOL

These posters are all down the corridor.

And they're in the next corridor too. Carl told me this morning when I met him that Walton has given permission for candidates to put up as many posters as they like until the election on Friday. But with the amount of LEJEUNE posters that are already stuck up there isn't going to be any room for anybody else's. Mind you, I can't see that anybody's going to notice Carl's lousy poster up against all the LEJEUNE ones. All his posters are just bigger versions of the leaflet he gave me yesterday on paper that's about as flimsy as the stuff you get in toilets. The LEJEUNE posters are on really high-quality shiny stuff and they look good. At first I think they're all the same but then I notice differences. One says,

> VOTE   LEJEUNE
> HE'S   THE   MAN

Another,

> VOTE   LEJEUNE
> HE'S   HOT

Another one,

                    VOTE LEJEUNE
           DO YOURSELF A FAVOUR

And,

                    VOTE LEJEUNE
           THE MAN WITH A PLAN

There are probably other messages too but I don't get to see them because I've got to start putting my plan into action. Carl told me he was having problems with three things: his posters, his friends and his grades in History. I haven't worked out how to do anything about the last two. I can't see his friends liking it much if I walk up to them and say, 'Why aren't you talking to Carl?' They're in Year Eleven, they'd probably hit me. And I don't really see the point of finding out who his History teacher is and asking if I could have a quick word because I am worried about Carl's grades. I'm not his mum and the teacher would probably notice.

Which leaves me with one option. The posters. My idea is to put a poster up and then see if it gets torn down. This will tell me if Carl is imagining it all. It's not much of a plan but I haven't got that much time and

I've got to start somewhere. So, I find one of the few bits of wall that hasn't got a VOTE LEJEUNE poster on it and stick up one of Carl's. I was right. It doesn't look good. Even though it's got things written on it that I think would be good ideas, I'd still rather look at the others. They're shiny and they've got a picture.

I tear myself away and head into French. An hour and ten minutes later, after Miss Hardy has tried for the one millionth time to teach us about the past tense and only succeeded in getting herself all red and upset, I'm out again.

The poster is gone.

None of the LEJEUNE posters have. At least, not as far as I can tell. There's so many of them that it's not too easy.

Still, I've got to give it to Carl. Something might just be going on. I need to put the next part of my plan into action. Trouble is, I don't actually know what the next part of my plan is. But it's break so I've got twenty minutes to work it out. I head off down to the canteen to get a Coke and a packet of crisps to help me think.

Twenty minutes later I've got a plan. I'm not saying I like it but I've got one. What I need is to be able to watch the corridor and spot whoever rips the poster down. There are two problems with this. If I stand watching then the person who's going to rip the poster down might see me and change his mind. And on top of that I'm supposed to be in English.

The first one's not too hard to work out. I just stick the poster up in one corridor and watch from round the corner. The second is harder. I've got to be in English. If I don't go the morons at the back or Katie Pierce will grass me up and Miss Hurley's the kind of teacher who checks the register and rings your parents. That's the kind of efficient teaching I could do without right now. So, I've got to find a way to be in the corridor and yet not miss English. There's only one way of doing that I can think of and that's to get sent out. I haven't got time to work out how so I stick one of Carl's posters up in the Maths corridor, which is next to the English corridor, and run to Miss Hurley's lesson.

'Mickey, you're late,' she says as I come through the door.

'Am I?' I say.

'Yes.'

'Should I stay outside the classroom for the whole lesson as a punishment?'

'Don't be stupid. Go and sit down and be here on time next lesson.'

Perhaps I was a bit obvious.

I go and sit down. There's this poem on my desk. I pick it up. It's called 'Ozymandias'. It looks boring so I put it down again. I try to work out what's the best way to get thrown out of a lesson. The difficult thing is getting yourself into the right kind of trouble. Anyone can get themselves thrown out of a class just by walking up to the teacher and punching him on the nose. But that would not only get you thrown out of class, it would also get you thrown into the Head's office and then get you thrown straight out of school. That's not the kind of trouble I'm aiming for.

Not having done your homework's no good. That gets you a detention. Not listening isn't good enough either. Teachers pretend they care about whether you're listening or not but they don't really. What they care about is whether you're talking or not. If you sit through a lesson and never listen to a word the teacher says but never actually do any talking either, they don't do anything.

I should know. I've been doing it for most of this year.

No, the way to get yourself thrown out of a class is to be irritating but not irritating enough to get you sent to your Head of Year. It's a fine line and I've got to walk it. I pull a rubber out of my pocket and wait for the right moment.

'Now,' says Miss Hurley, 'look at the poem –

I met a traveller from an antique land
Who said: Two vast and trunkless legs of stone
Stand in the desert.

'What does the poet mean by "trunkless"?'

'Is it something to do with elephants?' asks the Thick Girl with Glasses who sits at the front.

'No,' says Miss Hurley.

'Is it like a car without a boot?' asks the Even Thicker Girl with Pigtails who sits next to her. They've got names but in three years I've never seen the point of learning them.

'Why do you say that?' asks Miss Hurley.

'The Americans call the boot of a car a trunk, don't they, miss?'

'But where's the car in this poem?'

'Oh.' The Even Thicker Girl with Pigtails looks down. You've got to feel sorry for the two of them. They've answered almost every question our class has been asked since we came to the school and I don't think they've ever got one right.

'Does "trunkless" mean he's forgotten to put his swimming costume on?' shouts out Katie Pierce.

'What?' says Miss Hurley.

'Well, he isn't wearing his swimming trunks, is he? That means he's naked,' explains Katie Pierce.

'You must be able to see his thingy,' says Julie Reece.

'Is this poem pornography?' asks Katie.

The morons at the back all pick up the poem for the first time and stare at it intently. They don't know many long words but 'pornography' is one of them.

'I don't think you should make us read pornography in class,' says Julie to try and wind Miss Hurley up.

'Is that what an "Ozymandias" is, miss?' asks Katie innocently. 'Is it an old word for penis?'

'Be quiet,' shouts Miss Hurley.

The class shut up immediately.

You've got to give it to Miss Hurley. With

most teachers once the words 'pornography' and 'penis' have appeared in a lesson they've got no chance of getting away with anything less than a riot. But Miss Hurley's different. There's something in her eyes that tells you she's not messing about. I can't explain it. You just have to look at her. She's not bluffing.

Miss Hurley stares at the class. The class stay quiet. This is my moment. I turn round and fling my rubber at the morons at the back. It hits one of them right on the nose. I retired from chucking things round classrooms when I left primary school but I've lost none of my touch.

'Owww!' shouts the moron at the back.

The two morons sitting next to him start laughing.

'Miss,' shouts the moron. They like to think they're hard, the morons, but if anything goes wrong they always run straight to the teacher.

'Yes?' says Miss Hurley.

She must have seen it. I couldn't have made it more obvious if I'd stood up in assembly and told everybody that's what I was going to do.

'Mickey Sharp just hit me with a rubber.'

'Did he?'

'Yes.'

'Did it hurt?'

'Er . . .' The moron's confused. If he says it didn't hurt then it sounds like he's moaning about nothing. But if he says it did hurt then he'll look like a wimp. After all, it's only a rubber.

The moron is stuck with two choices and he doesn't know which one to go for. The class waits for his decision. We could be here way into lunch time.

'Perhaps he's suffering from post-traumatic stress,' suggests Katie Pierce.

'Be quiet, Katie,' says Miss Hurley.

'I was only trying to—'

'Quiet.'

I'm looking at Miss Hurley. I don't get it. She must have seen it. Why's she not calling me on it?

'I'll tell you what,' she says to the moron. 'Put your head on the desk and rest your nose. I don't want to see your head raised for the rest of the lesson.'

'But what about him?' says the moron. He means me.

'I'll deal with him later,' says Miss Hurley. 'You put your head down and get better.'

You can see by the moron's face that he knows he's being made to look a fool. Putting your head on the desk is what they made you do at primary school. But you can also see that he can't work out how to get out of it. And so he puts his head on the desk. I glance back at Miss Hurley. She's smiling.

And then suddenly I get it. Miss Hurley clocked me chucking the rubber but she's not too bothered about that. She's just using it as an excuse to get one of the morons at the back to stay out of the lesson. Teachers can be so devious.

'Returning to "Ozymandias",' she says. 'A trunk is another word for torso. So, to be trunkless is to be without the middle of your body.'

A bit like the supermodels my sister's always looking at in magazines.

'Would anybody be prepared to hazard a guess as to the meaning of the word "visage"?'

I tune her out. I've got to get out of the classroom so I'm able to see who pulls the poster down. I reckon doing something stupid is the right idea. My problem was that I picked on the wrong person. I figure I'll go for the old pen-and-chair trick. It's so stupid that nobody does it out of primary school so there's a good chance it'll work. The only problem with it is that you need to do it on the person sitting in front of you. And the person sitting in front of me is Umair.

Umair used to be my best friend. But we kind of stopped. He's clever and he works hard and his parents want him to be a lawyer or a doctor. They think I'm a bad influence, which I suppose I am. But then so is Channel 5 and I don't see anybody banning that. Umair respects his parents, which shows he can't be that clever, and so, once they put the pressure on, we stopped hanging out. We never had a big fight or anything. It was just sort of gradual. I didn't really notice and then one day we weren't friends any more.

But that makes me a bit more reluctant to pull the trick on him.

Still, there's a case to solve and when you're a detective you can't start letting personal feelings get in the way of stuff.

I pick up my pen and chuck it so it lands on the floor at the side of his desk. Just out of reach. Perfect.

I tap him on the back. He turns round. He looks a bit annoyed. I suppose he was concentrating on the poem about the guy without a body.

'Pen,' I say and I point towards it.

He gets out of his chair and bends down to pick up the pen. He puts it back on my desk. I nod. He turns round and starts to sit down. I wait till he's committed and then whip the chair away with my legs. He falls on the floor. The class has a choice between studying some poem seriously or laughing at someone looking stupid. Guess which one they go for.

'What is going on over there?'

Umair picks himself up and looks at me. His expression is a mixture of anger and confusion. I try to show him by my face that it wasn't meant personally and that I had to do it. He doesn't look any less angry so I figure my face isn't up to it.

'Fool,' he says. And then he picks his chair up.

'Umair,' says Miss Hurley, 'what is the meaning of this?'

'Nothing, miss,' he says. Trust Umair. He's not going to grass me up. So now I feel even worse and I'm not going to get chucked out of class.

'Something happened,' says Miss Hurley. She's not the kind of teacher who lets things go. 'And I would like to know what it is, if you would have the courtesy to tell me.'

'I pulled Umair's chair away,' I tell her. If Umair's not going to grass me up then I'm going to have to do it myself.

'He threw a rubber at my nose too,' the moron at the back reminds everyone.

'Why, Mickey?'

'Dunno,' I tell her and I throw in a shrug for good measure.

If there's one thing that is guaranteed to drive teachers crazy it's saying 'dunno' and adding a shrug like you don't care. There's not a teacher in the world it doesn't work on and it can't let me down now.

'Well, Mr Sharp, you can go and stand outside the door of this classroom until you do know. Go on. Out.'

What did I tell you? It never fails.

CHAPTER 4

As soon as I've shut the door behind me I slip down to the Maths corridor to see if the poster's still there. It is. Now all I've got to do is wait for someone to rip it down.

I get back to Miss Hurley's door. She's not the kind of teacher you want to disappear on when they've sent you out. And I've got to get out of the Maths corridor to give whoever is ripping down the poster a chance to do it. My plan is that they'll pull it down and then come round the corner into the English corridor. I'll see them and remember their face and then as soon as they've passed me I'll slip down to the Maths corridor, see that the poster has gone and I'll be onto the kid who's tearing them down. At least it will be a start.

A girl turns into the English corridor from the Maths one. I check her face in case I need to remember it. Blond hair cut in a bob. Kind of round face. A few spots. Red glasses. Probably Year Ten. I wait until she's disappeared and then I check the Maths corridor for the poster. It's still there.

A bit later a boy comes past. He's tall and thin. Red hair, about a number two. And freckles. I'll be able to trace him. You can always find kids with red hair when you need to. I wait till he's gone and then check the poster again but it's still there.

I didn't need to remember either of them.

Then nothing happens for a while. And then it happens for a while longer. There's a little whirring noise above me. I look up. It's a camera moving. When we came back to school after the Christmas holidays there were CCTV cameras all over the place. The teachers say that it's for security reasons so that intruders in the school can be identified and intercepted sooner but I don't buy that. I bet Walton just likes spying on kids. He thinks every kid in the school is a potential criminal.

The door opens behind me. I figure it's Miss Hurley checking I've not run off but it turns out to be Katie Pierce. She looks at me like I'm a piece of dirt, which is normal, and then walks off. But she goes the Language corridor way rather than the Maths corridor way so she can't be after the poster.

Still nobody else has come past from the other direction. I'm tempted to check my watch to see how long I've been out there even though I know it's a mistake. To stop myself I decide to check to see if the poster's still there. I know it's got to be because nobody's been past but I glance round the corner anyway.

What I see gets me back outside the classroom as fast as I can go because what I see is Walton.

Just my luck. I get sent outside and the Head comes past. He's never been my biggest fan and he's not going to miss a chance like this. I think of running off and hiding in the toilets until he's gone but I can't risk it. If Miss Hurley comes out and finds I'm not there with him around then he'll have all the ammunition he needs to get my mum and dad back up to school. And the last time that happened things got ugly at home and I can do without that right now.

So, I stand outside the door and wait for him to come round the corner and give me a going over. It's funny though. When you know that you're going to get into trouble you just want it to happen as quickly as possible so you can carry on with your life.

But it seems like ages and Walton still hasn't appeared. I mean, I know he's old and everything but he should be able to walk faster than this. If it's taking him so long to get down a corridor then he should be seeing his doctor. Or maybe he's forgotten something and turned round and gone back the way he came.

Just when I'm thinking that, he comes round the corner. I stand by the classroom door and wait. He sees me. I look at him. His face looks weird. It's as if he's surprised, which is strange as seeing me stood outside a classroom is hardly a new thing.

'Sharp,' he says. His voice doesn't sound angry like normal.

'Yes, sir,' I answer.

'Sharp,' he says again.

'Yes, sir.'

'What are you doing out here?'

'Miss Hurley sent me out.'

'Did she? Did she? Well . . . er . . . don't do it again.'

And with that he walks past me and disappears down the corridor.

There are not that many things that can shock me any more. I'm fourteen. I've seen most stuff. But this? This is unbelievable.

No shouting. No criticism. No poking his finger in my chest. No detention. No threats to ring up my parents. No description of how my life will be a complete and utter failure because I neglected to apply myself in school and how I won't make any friends and I'll become ever more bitter and turn into a serial killer and spend most of my adult life in jail being beaten up every day by the other prisoners. Admittedly that last bit was on a day when he was particularly hot. You don't get that every time. But to get nothing . . . It's too weird.

I stand there for a while trying to explain it to myself – Walton passing up a chance to give me a good going over. He recognized me. He knew I'd been sent out. He did nothing. He must be ill.

And then I remember the reason I'm out here in the first place, which is the poster. I wander down the corridor to check it out.

But where the poster once was there's nothing but a space. It's gone. A little bit of paper stuck to a drawing pin is all there is to indicate it was ever there at all.

What a lousy detective I am. I've laid the bait, staked out the scene and then when

the bad guy comes along I'm too busy thinking about the health of my Head Teacher to
catch him. Some detective.

CHAPTER 5

So, the plan worked. Only I didn't. I'm still angry with myself an hour later. I nip into the toilets before heading over to the hustings or whatever stupid thing they're called to see if I can get a lead there. When you've got nothing much to go on you've just got to keep looking and hope you get a break.

I spend as little time as possible in the toilets. Some kid has bunged up all the sinks with toilet paper and left the taps running and there's water all over the floor. I don't get why kids do that. It's only messing it up for the rest of us. Teachers have their own toilets so it's not hurting them. I might even have switched the taps off but there are two Year Eleven kids sharing a fag and they'd see me. It's not worth risking your reputation to save a toilet.

I zip up and head outside. I've still got five minutes before the meeting starts so I'm in no rush.

'Excuse me.'

I'm stopped by a girl. I guess she must be Year Ten. At least, I hope she is because she's taller than me. She's standing right outside the boys' toilets, which is a bit weird. I mean, sometimes boys hang round the girls' toilets but girls never hang round the boys'. You can't blame them. It doesn't smell too good.

'Could you spare me a couple of minutes?'

'What for?'

'I'm Nicola Cohen from *Yell*.'

'What?'

'The school newspaper.'

I remember. We've got this school newspaper which comes out about four times a year. It's rubbish and nobody reads it. They start off trying to sell it for a pound and nobody buys it so the next week they try selling it for fifty pence and nobody buys it and then the next week they give it away to anyone who wants it and they've still got loads left at the end of it all. Every time a new one comes out they try selling it again as if nobody remembers that if you wait a couple of weeks then they'll be begging you to have one for free.

'So?' I say.

'We're conducting an opinion poll for

tomorrow's paper measuring voting intentions for the elections. Would you be prepared to tell me which way you'll be voting?'

'Tomorrow's paper?' I say. Normally the school newspaper's about six months behind. They cover sports day in December.

'Yes,' she says. 'We'll be publishing on Wednesday, Thursday and Friday. Only a two-page issue each day but the editor has got special permission to cover the election as it happens. We get out of lessons in the afternoon to write it.'

There's some strange people in the world. Imagine getting out of lessons just to do more writing.

'Are you prepared to let our readers know your voting intentions?'

Readers. She's confident. Like there'll be more than one.

I tell her I don't know who I'll vote for as Head Girl but I'll be voting for Carl Marks as Head Boy.

She makes a mark on her pad.

'Do you think he'll get many votes?' I ask. I might as well find out how my client's doing. I wonder if it's as bad as I expect.

'Oh, I couldn't tell you that,' she tells me

really seriously. 'That might compromise the paper's exclusive.'

Exclusive? She's really kidding herself. But I don't push it. I kind of like her. She's not like most girls in our school who check you out to see whether you're cool enough before they'll even think about talking to you.

'Why are you doing your survey outside a toilet?' I ask. 'Why not do it somewhere a bit less smelly?'

'I've got to get a balanced sample of respondents,' she says. 'If I do it in other places the sample might be biased. If I did it in the library you'd get too many dedicated students but if I did it on the field you'd get too many who were interested in sport. But everybody uses the toilet so it will be an accurate reflection of voter intentions.'

She talks a bit like one of those people that make me want to switch off the TV but she's got a point. Sooner or later everybody goes to the toilet.

And then I realize that I'm late.

'Hope it doesn't get too smelly for you,' I say and then immediately wish I hadn't. Talking about toilet smells isn't the best way to impress a girl. Not that I want to impress her. I'd just like not to make a fool of myself for once. That's the thing with girls. Something about them makes you say stupid things.

I head off to the sports hall before I go red. I flick a couple of glances back at her on my way. She's still stopping boys coming out, asking them what they think and writing things down in her pad. Some kids enjoy the strangest things.

When I get there it isn't exactly packed. There's maybe thirty kids and up on the stage there's Miss Gartree, who's one of the Deputy Heads, and sitting behind her are two girls and two boys. One of the boys is Carl. I figure the one next to him must be Tony Lejeune. Walton's talking. I lean against the wall and tune in.

'... That concludes the speeches and questions for the candidates for Head Girl. You must decide which one you will vote for. We now come to the candidates for Head Boy. There are two candidates, Tony Lejeune and Carl Marks. Each candidate has five minutes to explain their policies and ask for your vote and then you'll be able to ask them questions. First I call on Tony Lejeune.'

As soon as he stands up there's this wild applause. It comes out of nowhere. There's screaming and cheering and whoops. It's very strange. He's only some sad Year Eleven kid and they're acting like he's a pop star. But because there aren't that many of them it sounds really false like they think they ought to make the noise.

He goes up to the lectern thing that Walton stands behind at assembly and starts off.

'Friends,' he says. He's not my friend. 'Fellow pupils of Hanford High. I humbly come to you today to ask for your vote as Head Boy. Mr Walton has kindly trusted us to decide and I want you to repay that trust by voting for me. I will be a Head Boy to lead this school at the start of the new millennium, to modernize it and to make us feel good about it. Hanford High is a school that we should all be proud to attend. It has excellent teachers and wonderful facilities. I ask you to vote for me so that we can celebrate those great things and yet can also respond to the challenge of change. For today we stand on the edge of history and I am the boy to answer the call of history, if you can answer the call by voting for Tony Lejeune.'

The audience starts cheering. I start feeling sick. Lejeune waves to the audience, flashes them a toothy smile and goes back to sit in his place

Miss Gartree stands up. 'That was a very good speech, I think you'll agree,' she tells the audience.

Good speech? Excellent teachers and wonderful facilities? Celebrate the great things about Hanford High? There's more rubbish in there than there is in the landfill behind my gran's.

'And now,' says Miss Gartree. 'We have to hear from the second candidate.'

Carl stands up and shuffles towards the lectern. There's no noise at all as he prepares to speak. No claps, no cheers, no whoops. If it was just down to the people in the audience then I think it's fairly obvious who'd win.

'Hello,' he says. 'I'm Carl Marks. I think that school uniform is an interesting idea and I can certainly see that there are arguments for maintaining it because otherwise school might turn into a fashion show and I know that homework is important and we all have to do some and that individual showers cost a lot of money but—'

'Thank you, Carl,' says Miss Gartree from behind him.

Carl turns round. Miss Gartree grabs him by the shoulders and steers him back towards his seat.

'I'm afraid we're running short of time,' she tells the audience, 'but I'm sure that most of you got the basic idea of what Carl was saying, and if you didn't there's always the final hustings at Friday morning assembly before the vote takes place. Now, are there any questions?'

About ten hands go up. Miss Gartree points at one.

'Yes.'

'This is for the guy who spoke last,' says a voice which I recognize straight away. What is Katie Pierce doing here? She should be hanging out with her gang on the far side of the field chain-smoking like she always does.

'Are you a geek?'

The audience roars with laughter. Carl goes a bit red.

'I don't think that's a very fair question,' says Miss Gartree. 'Nobody's going to admit to being a geek. Any more questions?'

She points at one of the raised hands. It's a boy next to Katie.

'This is also for the guy who spoke last,' he

says. 'Is it true that you don't have any friends?'

The audience laughs again. Carl goes redder.

'I don't really think it's appropriate to ask people questions about their personal life,' Miss Gartree says. 'And I'm sure Carl has got one or two friends, haven't you, Carl?'

Miss Gartree looks at Carl. Carl's got his head in his hands he's so embarrassed by everything.

'Perhaps not,' says Miss Gartree. 'Still, that's all we've got time for today. Remember to vote on Friday. Hanford High needs a Head Boy that we can all respect.'

'And Head Girl,' says one of the girls behind her.

'Of course,' says Miss Gartree quickly. 'Of course. Now back to class because lunch time's nearly over.'

The kids start to leave the hall. I look at my watch. There's still fifteen minutes before the bell goes.

There's something weird going on.

CHAPTER 6

UNANIMOUS SUPPORT FOR LEJEUNE, SAYS POLL

It's the next morning and I'm reading a copy of the school newspaper. They're not even bothering trying to sell it this week. They're giving it away at all the entrances to the school. They're practically forcing it on people as they come in. And it doesn't look good for my client.

Handsome Tony Lejeune (Year 11) looks set for a landslide victory in Hanford High's first ever election for Head Boy. A representative sample of school public opinion unanimously supported Lejeune's bid for the top job. One source close to Lejeune exclusively told this reporter, 'We're delighted with the results of your poll but we would urge our supporters not to take victory for granted. It's important that they remember to vote on Friday.' The poll makes grim reading for Carl Marks, who is opposing Lejeune.

100% of those polled supported Lejeune whilst 0% supported him. Marks refused to comment on the result but seasoned observers consider it unheard of for someone to overturn such a massive lead and believe Marks's chances of victory are now as dead as the fish in the school aquarium.

by Nicola Cohen (10B)

Also in this issue:

HEAD GIRL'S RACE TOO CLOSE TO CALL *by Kelvin Sleazer (11E)*
WHY COOL KIDS WEAR PERFECT SCHOOL UNIFORM *by Kelvin Sleazer*
PUPILS IN YEAR 10 DEMAND MORE HOMEWORK *by Kelvin Sleazer*
MR WALTON SAVES BABY FROM BURNING BUILDING *by Kelvin Sleazer*

I chuck it on the floor. I've never read the school newspaper before and I'm never going to read it again. It's rubbish. And it'll probably lose me a case. Once Carl gets an eyeful of the opinion poll results he'll sack me as quick as he can. Who cares whether the odd poster is going missing when you're getting results like that?

And then I pick the paper up again and flick to the story about Walton and the baby. I know it's got to be rubbish but I can't stop myself looking at it. Like children's TV on Saturday mornings.

MR WALTON SAVES BABY
FROM BURNING BUILDING

Mr Walton, the popular Head Teacher of Hanford High, was universally commended yesterday when it emerged that he had saved a child from near certain death on his way home from work only three days ago. Eagle-eyed and ever alert, Mr Walton MA spotted a garden shed which had caught fire in mysterious circumstances. Nearby he spied a lady pushing a pram down the street. The pram contained a baby. Mr Walton rushed up to the lady. 'Don't take the baby into that garden shed,' he ordered powerfully. 'It's on fire.' The lady obeyed the order from Mr Walton, which will come as no surprise to teachers and pupils at Hanford High, where he is renowned as a natural leader, and disaster was averted. When interviewed, Mr Walton was as modest as ever. 'It's what any brave, alert, publicly minded citizen would have done,' he said. He went on, 'If only people didn't drop litter there wouldn't be any fires.' A point well made by Hanford High's own have-a-go hero.

I have to read the story twice it's so unbelievable. The only thing that sounded like it could be true at all was Walton going on about litter. And then, just when I'm thinking about how many mistakes there are in this story, it suddenly crashes into my mind that there was a big mistake in the other one. I flick back to the first page. '100% of those polled supported Lejeune whilst 0% supported him.' Him being Carl Marks. Except that I was polled and I supported Carl Marks. Maths isn't my best subject but I know that 0% means no votes. And he got mine. Maybe that girl outside the toilet wasn't as straight as I'd figured. I need to find her and throw a few tough questions her way. Fast.

The bell goes, which is bad news. That means I've got to get registered before I can go and find her. It's a pain being at school when your main job is being a detective. Things keep distracting you.

I could just skip registration but Newman's going to be hot on late detention this week after his big stress with Katie Pierce yesterday so I decide not to risk it. I'll just stick my head round the door, say I'm in and tell him that I've got to see a teacher about some homework. It normally works if you don't do it too often.

I get to our form room. Newman's in there tidying up his desk and ignoring the rest of the class. He's always going on at us about being organized but he isn't any better. He's always losing stuff and his shirt's always creased.

'Sir,' I say.

'Not now,' he snaps back without looking up.

'Sir, I need to go and see Ms Walter about some homework.'

'Wait a minute.'

Never stop when you want a favour from a teacher. They're much more likely to say yes if they're distracted. Give them time to concentrate and your chances go through the floor.

'Sir, I'm going to see Ms Walter. She said I've got to. Mark me in, yeah?'

'You're going nowhere. Sit down.'

'But . . .'

'I said sit down. It's litter pick this morning

62

and I need every one of you here. Mr Walton was very disappointed with the amount of refuse we managed to collect last time. We were bottom of the whole of Year Nine.'

There's a big groan from the rest of the class when he says that it's litter pick. It's one of the worst things that they make you do in school. Nobody wants to touch some of the stuff that's lying around on our field.

I walk over to my chair and sit down. As soon as I do three rubbers hit me in the face. The morons at the back have picked the time to get their revenge.

'*There* it is!' shouts Newman, pulling a big black bin bag out of one of his drawers. 'Right, everybody. Down to the playground as quickly as you can.'

Typical. He spends all this time getting me to sit down just so I can get three rubbers in my face and then I've got to stand up again.

Nobody moves particularly fast on the way down. Picking up litter is never going to be the sort of thing that gets the adrenaline going. This guy came to talk to us once. He said he was a greenie or something. He said that we should look after the earth because it was the only one we've got and that whenever he saw a piece of litter at work, even if he hadn't dropped it, he picked it up. And then he looked really pleased with himself. The thing is, he looked like the kind of guy who worked in an office with a whole lot of other greenies and they probably never drop any litter so they never have to pick any up. It's easy for him. You start trying to pick up every piece of litter you saw at our school and you'd never get to a single lesson. And then they'd expel you. It's a no-win situation.

By the time we get down there all the playground's already been nicked by other Year Nine forms. It's best to pick there because that's where the bins are. All you do is grab the bag, nip off to a bin and empty it into your bag. Then you've got a whole load of rubbish and nobody has had to pick anything up. The teachers know the kids do it but whenever they see that it's about to happen they look the other way. They hate litter pick almost as much as we do.

So that means we've got to pick on the field, and because even the near bits of the field are taken we've got to walk right over to the far side. It must have rained pretty hard last night because the ground's all wet, which makes the whole litter pick thing even less appealing and it didn't have many fans before.

'Right then, let's get started,' says Newman enthusiastically.

You've got to admire teachers sometimes. Newman knows full well that none of us are going to pick up any litter but he makes his voice sound like he's just offered us all the chance to pick up free computer games rather than soggy chocolate wrappers and empty crisp packets.

'I can't bend down,' Katie Pierce tells him. 'I've hurt my coccyx.'

'So've I,' echoes Julie Reece.

'And us,' add the rest of Katie's gang.

'Us too,' shout the morons at the back.

Within five seconds the class have all claimed the same injury that prevents them bending down, which means none of them can do the litter pick. Newman puts down his empty bag and stares at us.

'Look,' he says. 'I know this isn't the best job in the school. I know that some of you don't want to do it. I know that you feel it's a bit much to ask. But if we all work together as a team, as a form, as a group, then we'll get it done in no time. Let's not see this as a litter pick. Let's see this as a team challenge.

Our form. Up against all the other forms in Year Nine. Can we beat them? Yes, we can. Let's go.'

There are times when you forget that Newman's a new teacher and then he goes and reminds you by saying something dumb like that. Everybody looks at him. Nobody moves.

'Come on,' he says, trying to smile like he's our friend or something. 'Come on.'

It's embarrassing to watch. The whole class just stands there. He's losing face by the second. He holds his smile but it starts to look more like he's in pain.

I can't look at him any more. It's stupid, but it's like he's let me down. When you get a new teacher like Newman they're always rubbish at first and they always pretend it isn't their first job but you always know. They've got this look like they're clean and they believe in stuff and they're always leaving their wallet lying around. And then they realize what it's really like and you start to see whether they're going to be any good or not. And I thought Newman had a shot. I thought he might not be that bad a teacher. And then he starts talking about a litter pick as a team challenge. It's like he's gone backwards.

I leave him to it and wander off towards the far fence where our field ends. Nobody notices because Newman's still trying to sell the litter pick as a big fun thing and the rest of the form aren't buying. Apart from the Thick Girl with Glasses and the Even Thicker Girl with Pigtails, who'd believe anything a teacher told them and start picking up litter like mad. They probably still believe Father Christmas comes down the chimney and that being in Special Needs really means you're special.

I get to the fence and look out onto the waste ground behind. You're not supposed to go on it because there's some poisonous gas underneath it or something. My dad's always moaning on about how they should clean it up but they never do. And then I notice something on the other side. It's a big black pile of smoking paper like someone's had a fire. That's not exactly unusual. Kids are always having fires round here. But what is unusual is that the wind picks up one of the bits of paper and carries it over the fence. It drops down next to me and I pick it up. It's all charred round the edges but you can still read a bit of it. It says 'NARROW LE' on it. I don't get that. I know that 'le' has something to do with French but I've forgotten what it means.

'Look – Mickey's picking stuff up. Come on, the rest of you.'

I turn round. The whole class is looking at me. I shove the paper into my pocket.

'Well done, Mickey,' says Newman.

'I wasn't—' I start.

'One credit. Now let's follow his example.'

I can't believe it. He thinks I'm litter picking. All the class think I'm litter picking. He's given me a credit. I haven't had a credit since Year Seven. Already the morons at the back are making sucking noises. He's destroying my reputation.

CHAPTER 7

I've got to wait until break to find Nicola Cohen. I spend most of Religious Studies ignoring the morons at the back who keep chucking paper on the floor by my desk and asking me to put it in the bin because I like picking up litter so much. You'd think they'd get bored with this joke after five minutes but the morons have a high boredom threshold, and they manage to keep going for the whole lesson.

I'm out of that classroom as soon as the bell goes for break. I don't really know where to find Nicola Cohen so I start off by checking all the toilets in the school. I figure if she was there yesterday she might be there today. I whizz round them all fast. There's no sign of her.

Not finding Nicola outside the toilets with a notepad, I'm a bit stuck for ideas. It's one of the things I'm always getting wrong as a detective. I think people are going to be where I want them to be. And then they're not. It can be very frustrating.

But then I get lucky. I remember the newspaper office. You wouldn't call it an office unless you were someone who worked out of a shed like I do. Really it's the room where the caretaker used to sit and smoke and do no work until last year. You could get cancer just walking down the stairs to it. But this year they've kicked the caretaker out and they've turned it into the school newspaper office.

I go down the Humanities corridor and head down the stairs. You can still smell the cigarette smoke. It'll probably take about a century to get rid of that. A bit like that nuclear waste in Russia that our Geography teacher's always going on about.

At the bottom of the stairs there are just two doors – one into the boiler room and one into the newspaper office with *EDITOR: KELVIN SLEAZER* written on it. I knock and walk in. There's this one kid sitting in there. He's big and he's got his feet up on the desk and he's talking into a mobile phone. He doesn't seem to notice me so I stand in the doorway feeling stupid.

'Monster,' he says down the phone. 'Monster! We'll do the interview with you this afternoon. And then we'll give you the front page tomorrow. It'll be monster, I'm telling you. Mon-mon-monster. Gotta go.'

He's got some kind of accent but what it is won't quite click into place even though I know I've heard it before. He looks up at me.

'G'day,' he says. 'What d'you want, mate?'

He's Australian. I didn't know we had any Australians in our school.

'Hurry up, mate,' he tells me. 'I got deadlines, you know.'

'Hi,' I say.

'Let's skip the intros, mate. What do you want? I'm busy, mate.'

I wish he'd stop saying mate all the time.

'I'm looking for someone,' I tell him.

'Who, mate?'

'Nicola Cohen?'

Something flashes across his face when I say the name but it's gone so quick that I don't know what it is.

'Slinky, sexy Nicky? Hey, mate, what boy isn't looking for her?'

I'm not sure we've got the same girl. The Nicola Cohen I'm talking about stands outside boys' toilets looking serious and asking questions.

'Er . . .' I say. I'm not doing too well in this

conversation. I blame his accent. Because all of the Australians I've ever seen have been on soaps that my sister watches I keep expecting him to tell me that his brother's been killed in a car crash or his sister's been secretly married or his dad's got a new job and the whole family's going to move to Perth when you know that really their acting contracts are up and they've all been sacked.

'Maybe you're too young to notice,' he says. 'But take my advice, little mate. Next time you see Nicky you check her out. If she lightened up she'd have a great future as a model.'

That really annoys me. When some kid in Year Eleven starts playing the big man just because he's two years older than you.

'Do you know where she is?' I say. I say it pretty tough too because he's getting on my nerves.

'No, I don't, mate. And I got things to do. So, get out of my office, will you?'

'But she writes for the paper. It's import—'

'Look, mate. I said I'm busy, all right? Now, don't make me come over there and kick you out. All right?'

I said my thing pretty tough. He says his thing really tough. That's just the way you can say things when one of you's big and in Year Eleven and when the other one's not and in Year Nine. The conversation's over. I bang the door on my way out to show I'm not scared but I'm not fooling anyone.

By the time I'm out of there it's five minutes until the end of break and I haven't got anywhere. And I need to start making some progress. With only two days to go before the big election I don't have time to waste.

CHAPTER 8

I'm due a bit of luck and normally when I'm due a bit of luck what I actually get is a lecture off my dad, a detention off a teacher and an 'E – must try harder' in French.

But surprisingly, this time I'm due a bit of luck and I get it.

I come out onto the playground and I see Nicola straight away. She's sitting on one of the benches by the tennis court. Or at least what was once a tennis court before someone chopped up the net with a knife and painted extra lines all over it so that nobody has got a hope of knowing what's in or out any more.

I get over there fast and sit down next to her. She doesn't look up. In fact, she hunches down even more.

'Hi,' I say.

She doesn't say anything.

'You interviewed me about the election yesterday, remember? Outside the boys' toilets.'

She still doesn't say anything.

'I made a joke about the smell.'

I wish I hadn't said that. It wasn't a good joke when I said it and now I'm reminding her of it. Cool, Mickey. Very cool.

'I just need to ask you a question about the article and then I'll go,' I tell her.

Sometimes you have to give girls a bit of encouragement to talk to you. And the only piece of encouragement I can think of is that I'll get out of her way if she does. Which isn't good if you think about it.

'What I wanted to ask you was about the article in the school newspaper. The poll figures weren't right because I said that I'd vote for Carl Marks but in the—'

'I didn't write it.'

She speaks. OK, she's lying but at least she's talking.

'Yes, you did. Your name's on it. And you did the poll. I was there.'

She laughs. But it's not a laugh that's got any humour in it. It's bitter and sarcastic just like my dad's when I ask him if I can have a new bike.

'Don't believe everything you read,' she says.

I don't believe everything I read. If I did

I'd be really depressed about my grades.

'Look,' I say, 'if it's to do with messing up the article then don't get too stressed. I'm no good at Maths. It's easy to get figures wrong.'

'Wrong?' She looks at me. Her face is really angry. 'I got things right. And I've still lost my job. After two years' hard work.'

'What job?' I say. I don't get it. One minute she's talking about getting things right in the article and now she's talking about losing her job. She's going all over the place. 'Was it a paper round?' I ask.

'What?'

'Waitressing?'

'What are you going on about?'

'The job you got sacked from.'

'I didn't lose a job like that. I lost my job at the school newspaper.'

This really knocks me back. How can you lose a job at the school newspaper? They're always begging people to help.

The bell goes.

'Why?' I ask.

'I've got to go to my lesson.' She picks up her bag.

'Just tell me why,' I say desperately.

'Why should I?' she says, standing up.

'You're just a dumb Year Eight kid and it's none of your business.'

I decide this is not the right moment to point out that I'm in Year Nine but my growth spurt's late. But I can't let her go. So far she's my only lead in this case.

'I'll walk with you,' I say. 'Tell me on the way.'

'Get lost,' she says. She stands up and starts walking off. This is not good at all.

'I'll get you your job back,' I shout after her.

She stops. Then she shakes her head and starts walking again. Then she turns round. 'How?' she says when she gets back to the bench.

'You talk to me and I'll talk to you,' I tell her. You don't often get to say stuff like that and I kind of enjoy it.

'This better be worth it,' she says. 'I've got double science now and I'd rather be there.'

She knows how to hurt, this girl. Comparing me unfavourably with science. Still, it makes me feel better about promising to get her job back when I haven't got a clue how I'm going to do it.

Now I've got her to talk, the next problem is where we're going to talk. We can't just stay outside on the bench. The playground's pretty much cleared of kids already and we'd be spotted by a teacher who'd want to know why we weren't in a lesson. Privacy is not one of the things that schools are big on. If you want to go for a chat where nobody else can see you, you've really only got one option and that's the toilets. I can't ask a girl to go into the boys' toilet. She's not used to the smell and it might kill her. So, it will have to be the girls'.

But there's still something about going into a girls' toilet that makes you feel wrong. It's a bit like when a policeman stares at you and you think you're about to be arrested for some big crime even though you know you haven't done anything. Still, the difference isn't as much as I'd expected. There's loads of graffiti and it doesn't smell of roses. I begin to feel more comfortable.

We duck into a cubicle and shut the door in case any teacher sticks a head in. I've never been in a toilet with a girl before so I try and do the right thing and leave the toilet seat for her to sit on. My gran would be proud of me. She's always saying I don't have any manners.

'So,' I say, 'tell me about the poll.'

'Tell me how you're going to get my job back,' she counters.

'Tell me about the poll first.'

There's a silence. We stare at each other. I've never really looked at her before. Her eyes are dark and sharp and her lips are pursed together. Her hair's cut in this long bob. She looks tough and she looks good.

'Listen,' I say. I tell her everything about the case and about Carl Marks and about how I think something weird is going on.

'This could be a great story,' she says.

'Hey,' I tell her, 'this isn't a story. It's a case. I didn't say you could write this. What about my client's confidentiality?'

'You didn't say it was off the record,' she shoots back. 'Anyway, there's no story and no case unless we get some evidence instead of standing in a toilet. It's in both of our interests to work together on this and decide what to do about it later.'

She's got a point. It's just I've never worked with anybody on a case before. I'm not sure I want a partner. But I've already told her everything and she's told me nothing. I haven't got much choice.

'OK,' I say. 'So tell me what you know.'

And finally I get somewhere. It's like this.

The school newspaper was run by her and this other kid, Alston, who was the editor. Walton told Alston that he wanted them to run an issue every day before the election keeping the kids informed. So they decided to do the poll. The result was really close – 55% for Lejeune and 45% for Carl Marks. They were just about to print it off when Alston gets called into Walton's office. Walton tells him it's about time someone else edited the newspaper and he's got this other kid to do it – Kelvin Sleazer. Alston tells Nicola that when he asked Walton why he was sacking him in this really important week, Walton said he'd spoken to Alston's teachers and they all said he was falling behind on his GCSE coursework and so he had to give up the paper because exams must come first. Sleazer tells Alston he wants to make changes and have more gossip and pictures because that's what kids want and not boring reports on sports day and the school play. Alston tells Nicola about this and she goes mad because she thinks that Sleazer will drag the paper downmarket. She's never even met Sleazer but she hears enough from Alston to make up her mind she doesn't want to work with him. She writes a letter saying that she resigns and leaves it on his desk.

This is where things get really stupid. I tell her that she doesn't need me to get her job back – she should just say she didn't mean to resign. She says it's not as simple as that. She wants a guarantee that nobody will interfere with anything she writes. So I've not only got to get Kelvin Sleazer to ask her to come back. I've also got to get him to say that he won't change anything she writes. I've got no idea how I'm going to pull that off but I decide that now is not the time to mention it. Still, her story checks out all right. The piece of paper with 'NARROW LE' that I found during the litter pick was a bit of the headline of her original article – 'NARROW LEAD FOR LEJEUNE'. What I need to know is how and why that story came to be junked and replaced by one that gave Lejeune a 100% poll rating. But there's still one problem with her story.

'Why was your name on the article this morning then?' I ask. 'Why wasn't it Kelvin Sleazer's? He's taken over the paper. He should have written it.'

She gives me this stare that doesn't look too friendly. I suppose after telling me every-thing that's going down she's not too happy to find that I'm still not sure I believe her completely. But she makes a big effort and sees it's a fair question and gives me the answer.

'He didn't find out until late yesterday that he was the new editor so he must have been very rushed getting the paper ready and left my name in by mistake.'

I'm not so sure this is the best explanation I've ever heard but I'm not going to dwell on it because bigger things are going off in my brain. For once I figure it out straight off. And it's so big it almost knocks me over. Who was the last person I saw near the poster before it disappeared? Who was at the hustings and saw it all get managed so unfairly? Who sacked Alston as editor of the school newspaper just before it could publish a poll showing that Carl Marks might become Head Boy? Who appointed a new editor? Who stands to gain most if Tony Lejeune gets elected rather than Carl Marks because then he won't have somebody demanding the abolition of school uniform and the installation of individual showers?

Walton. My Head Teacher. The man who stands up at assembly and tells us all that we should always do our best and never cheat.

He's guilty. He's rigging the school elections.

'I can't believe it,' I say. 'I know who did it.'

'Who?' Nicola says.

'This is amazing,' I tell her.

'Come on!' She really wants to know.

'Unbelievable!'

'Yes?'

'Fantastic!'

'Yes?'

'Amazing!'

'Who is in that toilet?'

Gartree. I'd know her voice anywhere. I got so excited about knowing who was guilty that I forgot to listen for the door. We're busted. Unless . . .

I jump for the toilet seat. If I can get my legs out of sight then maybe she won't know I'm there when she looks under. There's only one problem with the plan. Nicola has the same idea. We bang into each other. I fall back against the side of the cubicle. Nicola isn't so lucky. She slips on the floor. Her hands fly out trying to balance her but it's too late. Her head thumps against the side of the toilet and she slumps onto the floor. She doesn't move.

CHAPTER 9

'Well, Sharp. I've known you to be many things. Lazy, rude, uncooperative, ignorant, unpleasant. All of them. Not to mention inattentive, slovenly, unpunctual, immature. As well as demotivated, unhelpful, deceitful and cowardly.'

It's ten minutes later. I'm in Walton's office and I am in more trouble than I have ever been in my life.

'But even I, Sharp – even I would not have thought you were capable of this. To hide in the girls' toilets, to wait until a girl came in, to assault her and render her unconscious. In thirty years of teaching I haven't come across anything so disgusting. I am speechless.'

'But—' I start.

'You'd just better hope that girl is all right, Sharp. I'll expel you whatever happens but you'd just better hope that she recovers because if she doesn't … if she doesn't you'll be in a young offenders' institution until you're not young any more. Do you understand that, Sharp?'

'But it was an accident,' I blurt out. I've got to admit I'm getting very nervous. They got me out of there pretty fast but she wasn't dead. She wasn't moving but she was going to be OK. It was only a toilet. She can't be . . .

'You would say that, wouldn't you, Sharp? But lying comes as easy to you as breathing to the rest of us.'

'But, sir—'

'Shut up, lad.' Walton picks up this file from his desk. 'Do you know how many A grades at GCSE Nicola was predicted? Seven, Sharp. Seven. We don't have many students in this school who are going to get seven A grades. A pupil with a future, Sharp. A pupil whose performance would reflect well on the school. A pupil who could have helped this school move off the bottom of the league tables. And what do you do? You smash her head against a toilet. You had to assault an intelligent pupil, didn't you? You couldn't be satisfied with a girl who's going to get Gs and Us. God knows, there's enough of them about.'

'Honest, sir, I didn't assault her. She just slipped.' I'm getting really frightened now.

The thing is, I know Walton's mad. Most of the kids in our school know Walton's mad. But the rest of the world doesn't know. And I can just see him standing in a courtroom and telling a jury that I'm a murderer. He's a Head Teacher. They'd believe him.

'Save your whining for the police, Sharp. I don't want . . .'

He stops halfway through his sentence because the door opens and in comes Miss Gartree. Behind her is Nicola Cohen. I breathe the biggest sigh of relief I have ever breathed. She's alive. She's got a cut on the side of her head which she's holding a bandage to but apart from that she looks all right. She gives me a quick glance and then looks at the floor. And then I start to get worried again. Would she say I'd assaulted her just to get herself out of it? You never know with kids who aren't used to being in trouble. Because they haven't got any previous they get believed.

'Nicola,' says Walton as soon as he sees her, 'I'm so pleased you're all right.'

I've never heard Walton's voice sound like that before. Like he cares.

'Does your head feel all right?'

Nicola nods.

'No loss of memory or IQ?'

Nicola looks confused.

'Mr Walton,' Miss Gartree says, 'Nicola needs to tell you what happened.'

'Yes, Miss Gartree,' says Walton a bit irritably. 'Well, get Sharp out of here first. We don't want him intimidating her.'

'I—'

'Shut it, Sharp.'

There's the voice I know.

'I think Sharp should stay, Mr Walton,' says Miss Gartree.

'But,' says Walton, looking confused.

'Nicola's told me that what happened in the toilets was an accident.'

'She doesn't mean that. She's suffering from post-traumatic stress. She's predicted seven A grades, Miss Gartree. She wouldn't be voluntarily in a toilet in lesson time with a no-hoper like Sharp.'

'Nicola,' says Miss Gartree.

Everybody looks at her.

'It was an accident, sir,' she says. 'We tried to hide when Miss Gartree came in and we banged into each other and I slipped and hit my head.'

Phew. I am out of trouble. He can't expel me and he can't call the police just for bunking a lesson even if I was in the girls' toilets.

'But,' says Walton. You can see his whole world falling apart. He's been trying to get something really big on me for ages. And now, just when he thought he'd got it, it disappears like our music teacher's sanity on a Friday afternoon. 'But what were you doing in there with Sharp?'

'Mr Walton . . .' says Miss Gartree and she nods her head to the far corner of his office. Walton follows her over there. He walks like a broken man. But not as broken as he'll be when I prove that he's trying to rig the contest for Head Boy. One of us might be leaving this school but it isn't going to be me.

They have this whispered conversation. I figure they must be deciding what punishment we're getting. Gartree does most of the talking. Walton shakes his head and then he throws some ugly looks my way and then he shakes his head some more. I try to give Nicola an encouraging smile but she's staring down at the floor so she doesn't see it. She looks a bit upset. Still, she's probably never been in this situation before and she might not realize that the worst is over. I've been here loads of times and I figure that the most we can get now is a couple of detentions and maybe a letter home to our parents. I'll tell her how to intercept it.

There's a knock on the door and then the school secretary walks in.

'I've brought Tuesday's CCTV tape, Mr Walton,' she says.

'I'm busy,' he snaps. 'Leave it on my desk.'

It's good to know he's as rude to adults as he is to kids.

Walton and Gartree stop talking and come back over. Walton looks at us. He's seems to be about to say something and then he stops. And then he swallows. And then he stops again. He's not normally this slow. He enjoys it too much. I figure it must be because he's got to punish a star like Nicola.

'Miss Gartree . . .' Finally he gets started. 'Miss Gartree has told me a few things that have come back to her since the incident.'

What's he going on about?

'They slipped her mind in the initial moments when Nicola's safety was of paramount importance. But they have come back to her since. She tells me that when she went into the toilet she heard the two of you.'

I suddenly feel very tense. She's overheard me talking about the Head Boy thing. She's told Walton. Walton knows I'm onto him. This could get nasty.

'Miss Gartree tells me that when she came into the toilet she heard a boy's voice shouting, "Amazing!" and "Unbelievable!" and a girl's voice shouting, "Yes!" She has reached the obvious and unpleasant conclusion.'

He's really lost it.

'You were having sexual intercourse in that cubicle.'

CHAPTER 10

I thought I was unshockable. I've watched enough violent videos to be desensitized to most stuff. But having Walton ask me about sex! There's some things that you just can't prepare for. I feel myself going red. Very red. I look up at Walton. He's red. I look at Gartree. She's red. I can't look at Nicola. But then I don't need to because I can hear her.

'No, no, no, no, no.'

I think one 'no' would have been enough.

'How can you say something like that?' She sounds really upset.

'Now, now, Nicola, we had—' starts off Gartree but she doesn't get any further.

'And you, miss, suggesting it. It's horrible. It's disgusting.'

This is not doing my ego much good.

'Mr Walton, Miss Gartree, I want to make it clear that I did not have sexual relations with Mickey Sharp.'

'Well, we never really thought—'

'Yes, you did.'

'Well, Miss Gartree thought she heard—'

'How could you think that? How could you think that about me?'

She's getting hysterical. There are tears in her eyes. Her hands are clenched into tight fists. I can't believe it. Am I that ugly? If this is how girls respond to the thought of sex with me I don't think I'm ever going to have a family.

'Calm down, Nicola,' says Miss Gartree. 'Calm down.'

'Can I phone my dad, please?'

'What?' says Walton.

'Can I phone my dad? I want to tell him the horrible things you've been saying. I want to go home. I don't ever want to see this school again.'

It's getting worse. She's changing schools just because someone suggested she's had sex with me. Imagine if we really *had* done it. She'd emigrate to Australia.

'Now there's no need to be hasty,' says Walton.

'You're upset,' says Gartree.

'You've every right to be upset.'

'It's not a nice thing to think.'

'But we were concerned for your welfare.'

'Teenage pregnancy. Diseases.'

'We didn't do anything,' Nicola says again.

'No, no, we know,' says Walton.

'Nothing at all,' agrees Gartree.

'Can I phone my dad?'

'Nobody's stopping you phoning your dad, Nicola. Are they, Mr Walton?'

'No, Miss Gartree.'

'But perhaps, Mr Walton, it would be better if Nicola waits until she's calmed down before deciding to do that. What do you think?'

'She could sit in the library and think about it. Wait until she feels better.'

'She wouldn't want to upset her father and have him come rushing over. What does he do?'

'He works for the local paper.'

Walton's face goes white when she says that. 'The local paper,' he repeats.

'The local paper,' Gartree says after him. 'No, you certainly wouldn't want to upset him in a job as important as that.'

'Go and sit down in the library. Decide what to do when you're calm. That's best, isn't it, Miss Gartree?'

'Definitely, Mr Walton.'

'You'll go and get her when she's calmed down, won't you, Miss Gartree?'

'Of course, Mr Walton.'

'And then if you want to ring your dad, you can. So, if you want to go along . . .'

'What about him?' says Nicola. She means me. She says it like she hates me. That's just typical of kids who never get into trouble. As soon as they do they go over to the teacher's side.

'What about him?' says Walton.

'He'll just go and tell all his grubby little mates in Year Nine that we've been caught in the toilets and then he'll say what you said and then everyone will think what you thought and then everyone will be saying it and . . .'

She doesn't finish what she's saying because she starts sobbing. Mr Walton gets a tissue out of his pocket but it doesn't look too clean so he puts it away again. I wish someone would say something to defend me. I wouldn't go round spreading rumours about me and a girl if they weren't true. But it's pointless telling them. Nicola's in tears and Walton and Gartree are looking at me as if I've already posted the news on the ten most popular websites in the world.

'Mickey won't tell anyone,' says Walton.

But he doesn't say it in the kind of voice

that means 'Mickey won't tell anyone because he's a boy who doesn't go round spreading lies'. Instead he says it in the kind of voice that means 'Mickey won't tell anyone because I'll break his legs if he does'.

'Won't he?' sniffs Nicola. I'm beginning to get very sick of her.

'No, he won't. Mickey will go back to his lesson now and if he so much as breathes a word of this incident he'll be in detentions every night for a week, his parents will be called up to the school and he'll be on report for the rest of his natural life. So you won't say anything, will you, Mickey?'

They all look at me. This is one of those moments when every bit of you wants to say, 'I'll say what I want when I want and there's nothing you can do to stop me.' But this is the real world.

'No, sir.'

'No, sir,' Walton repeats in that smug voice all teachers use when they've made you say something you don't want to. 'All right, Nicola?'

Nicola sighs and sniffs and nods.

'Right,' says Walton. 'Back to class, Sharp. Nicola, you go for a nice sit down in the library until you feel ready to cope.'

'Can I wait until he's gone, sir?' says Nicola.

This is getting stupid. What is this girl on? It's the last time I have anything to do with kids who are going to get As. They're not worth the hassle.

'Of course,' says Walton. 'Off you go, Sharp.'

I walk out the door. But I'm not going straight to class. After what I've gone through I am going to wait in the corridor on the way to the library and when little Miss Goody-Goody-Cry-Baby walks by I am going to tell her how pathetic she is. And I don't care if she does tell Walton. Teachers can get away with humiliating you – it's the way the world works – but some teacher's pet girl in Year Ten? No way. I'm going to put her right on a few things.

I don't have to wait too long. Two minutes later I see her coming. She's wiping her eyes so she doesn't see me until it's way too late for her to turn back.

'What's your problem?' I say. She looks up. She looks surprised. 'Got to take it out on me, have you? Can't get into trouble as well. Can't have Mr Walton thinking you're not perfect.'

'Leave me alone,' she says.

'Why should I?' I say. 'You going to tell a teacher? You going to ring your dad?'

'Because,' she snaps back, 'if someone sees us together they might realize.'

'Realize what?' I throw back at her. This isn't how I meant it to be. I should be having a go at her, not asking her questions.

'That I was faking, you moron.' She raises her eyes to the ceiling. 'Didn't you get it?'

'Hey?' I seem to have spent most of this morning out of my depth.

'Mickey, we got caught bunking in the toilets. The girls' toilets. Together. A boy and a girl. And we've walked out without a punishment. Think about it.'

She walks off towards the library. I think about it. She turns round.

'Meet me behind the sports hall at lunch time. But be subtle about it. After this morning we can't afford to be seen together.'

She smiles at me and then she pulls a tissue out and makes her face look all sad. Then she turns round and heads into the library. I think about what's just happened some more. I should feel like a fool. And then I start smiling. I think I'm in love.

CHAPTER 11

French passes me by. It's been one hell of a morning and I'm in no mood for an emergency visit to a doctor who can't even speak English. I spend most of the lesson just staring out of the window. The morons manage to hit me on the head with rubbers at least three times but I hardly notice. I don't even notice when Miss Hardy asks me if anything's wrong or when Katie Pierce tells the whole class I've had a lobotomy. I'm too busy trying to think. This picture keeps coming into my mind of Nicola smiling and then suddenly making her face look sad.

When the bell goes I get moving fast. I'm round the back of the sports hall to meet her quicker than Miss Hardy can say, '*Vite*.' And what do I find? Nothing.

Well, unless you count eight million cigarette ends. It's funny when you think about it. The government spends loads of money building a sports hall to encourage kids to be active and healthy and instead kids use it as a big shield to smoke behind and make themselves really unhealthy. I bet it's the same in every school – build a sports hall and double the number of kids who smoke. If I'd listened in Maths in Year Eight, I could probably turn it into a graph.

I take one more shot at working out whether I'm going in the right direction in the case. The problem with being a detective is that it's too easy to try and pin the crime on the person you want to be guilty rather than the person who is. And I want Walton to be guilty more than anything. I check all the evidence again and it still points the same way. It has to be him. I can't wait to tell Nicola so I can get on with solving the case. This time it's personal.

But Nicola isn't the first person to come round the corner of the sports hall. Instead it's three boys from Year Eleven. And we're not talking any boys from Year Eleven. We're talking The Psychos.

The Psychos are the toughest gang in our school. There used to be about ten of them but there's only three left now because all the rest got expelled. The reason they got expelled is because they're so easy to catch. And the reason they're so easy to catch is because to be in The Psychos you've got to dye your hair blond and wear sunglasses. All the time. Which is why I've never had any trouble with them before. They're really easy to see coming and when you see them you just walk the other way.

But this is not an option now because one side of the sports hall is a dead end and the other way involves walking past them. Walking past The Psychos is the kind of thing that draws their attention. And when The Psychos give something their attention the next thing they do is give it a kicking. I'm trapped.

I lean against the sports hall trying to look like I'm not bothered. It's a tough call. You don't want to look too arrogant and cool because they'll take that as a challenge and smash your head in. But you don't want to look nervous or they'll take it as a sign of weakness and smash your head in. It's a narrow line to walk. Or to lean.

'Give us a fag.'

'You give us a fag.'

'Gave you a fag at break.'

'No you didn't.'

'Did, didn't I?'

'Don't remember.'

They're really great talkers, The Psychos. Still, I'm glad that they're obsessed with fags. It stops them noticing me. I just wish they'd get some in their mouths and then I could risk going past them. They won't bother you while they're smoking. They can only concentrate on one thing at a time.

'We're gonna have to buy some.'

'How much are they?'

'More than this.'

You'd think The Psychos would know how much a packet of fags costs.

'Oi.'

This is a bad 'Oi' because it's aimed at me. I turn round. They look so dumb with their dyed hair and their sunglasses. I'd laugh if they were on the TV. Trouble is, they aren't and I don't feel like laughing.

'Yeah,' I say. Don't look scared, I tell myself. You're dead if you look scared.

'You got any fags?'

'Nah.'

'You got any money?'

'Nah,' I say again. Keep it simple with The Psychos.

They start to move towards me. Don't back off, I tell myself. Don't look nervous. They stand around me. Close around me.

'You sure you ain't got no money?'

'Sure.'

'You saying I'm wrong?'

'I'm saying I ain't got any money.'

'Who do you think you are?'

'Nobody.'

'Give us your money.'

'Or we'll have to give you a slap.'

'A hard slap.'

'And a kick.'

'A good kick.'

'Understand?'

They get closer. This is one of those times when you wish that life was like the movies. That you could smash one of them in the face with your fist, drop kick another one and head butt a third. But this is real life. I stick my hand into my pocket, drag out a quid and hold it out.

'I just remembered,' I say.

One of them snatches it.

'Just remembered,' jeers another.

'We got enough for ten now.'

'Yeah.'

'Come on.'

They walk off. I feel like a coward. I feel like I should do something about it but there isn't anything I can do. Go and tell a teacher?

Don't make me laugh. The Psychos would all lie and say they didn't know what I was talking about and then they'd beat me up for grassing. Or they'd get suspended for a couple of days, come back and beat me up for grassing. Or they'd get expelled, wait outside the school and beat me up for grassing. Whichever way it goes I'd get beaten up.

'How come you were giving those boys money?'

I look up. It's Nicola. She must have seen what happened. This is worse. It's one thing giving in to The Psychos, it's worse to get seen. And it's even worse to be seen by the person you were hoping to impress.

'Where've you been?' I throw back. I'm angry with her for seeing me.

'Miss Gartree came to see if I was going to phone my dad. I had to tell her I was all right and I wasn't going to ring him. What about those boys?'

I don't want to get into it. It makes me look like such a wimp and girls don't like wimps. In PSE Ms Walter's always going on about how girls are more mature than boys because they don't just go on looks but really care about a boy's personality and whether he's sensitive and caring. All the girls go, 'Yeah,' when she says that. But they don't live it. Caring and sensitive boys get called wimps and I've never seen a wimp with a girlfriend.

'This was a dumb place to arrange to meet,' I tell her.

'Oh yeah?' she says. 'If I'd left it to you we'd both be sitting in a detention with Mr Walton.'

This is going wrong. I'd meant to get on with her but I just seem to be getting into an argument.

'All I'm saying,' I tell her, 'is there are better places.'

'I didn't know all the smokers came here,' she shoots back. 'You should have said.'

'You didn't give me a chance.'

'I was too busy getting us both out of trouble.'

'You don't need to keep going on about it.'

And then neither of us says anything for a while. This is turning into a disaster. We're supposed to be partners on this case and all we can do is shout at each other.

'Look,' I say, 'this is stupid. We've got to work out what to do next.'

'You still haven't told me who's behind it,' she says. 'And I can't help if I don't know.'

She's right. I'd forgotten that Gartree

interrupted us before I could tell her who was guilty. I don't waste any more time. 'It's Walton,' I say.

'Walton?'

I tell her why. I go through all the evidence. By the time I've finished I'm pretty impressed by my own theory. It all hangs together. He's got to be guilty. I'm a bit put out when she says, 'You're mad.'

'What?'

'He's a head teacher. He wouldn't do that kind of thing.'

'Look at the evidence.'

'What evidence? He might have been in a corridor when a poster was ripped down. Teachers don't do that sort of thing.'

'How do you know?' I fire back.

'Because they're teachers. They're adults. They aren't that stupid.'

If she thinks adults aren't stupid then she really is naive. Who started all the wars in the world? Who makes children's TV programmes? Who came up with the idea of school uniform?

'Who else could it be?' I ask her.

She shakes her head. 'Forget it,' she says. 'To think I got you out of trouble. To think I believed you when you said you'd get me my job back. And all you do is come up with that moronic idea. I thought you weren't like that. But you're just a stupid Year Nine kid. I'm going.'

And she turns round and walks off.

I can't believe it. I spend an hour thinking about a girl, get myself all set to impress her and then within five minutes she's decided I'm a moron and left. That's a world record even by my lousy standards.

And as I watch her go I realize that I haven't got an option. If I'm going to show her that I'm not a moron, I'm going to have to prove Walton's guilty. Prove it without the shadow of a doubt.

CHAPTER 12

But how do I prove it? I can't just walk up to
Walton and say, 'I know what you've been
up to. Admit it now and I'll put in a word
with the judge,' like the police do on those
cop shows.

I need to find a weak link. Not someone
who did anything wrong but someone who
knows the someone who did something
wrong and might talk. That's what they
always say on *Crimewatch*. Somebody knows
who did this crime and all they've got to do
is call. I run through my head all the people
who know something to see if they might
help. Walton – No. Lejeune – No. Kelvin
Sleazer – No. Nicola Cohen – Not any more.
There must be someone else. Someone else
who knows something. Someone I'm missing. There was something in what Nicola
said that I'm missing. After the poll and
before Kelvin Sleazer … The old editor of the
school newspaper. Alston. He got sacked by
Walton. He might be able to tell me

something that can help. Or he might not. But when you've got nothing, anything's an improvement.

Of course it's never easy. The first problem is that I don't know what he looks like. Nicola Cohen could tell me but I don't think she'll be feeling particularly co-operative. But I've got an idea for that one. The school secretary has a picture of every kid in the school in her office. You have to bring a new photo in every year to update her records. You give the name and she can show you the picture. The problem is coming up with a good reason to get her to show you the picture.

I want some progress before the end of lunch so I get round to the back door fast. There's a crowd of kids in the way so I start pushing through them. I get into the scrum but I can't seem to get out. Someone grabs my hand. I twist it but whoever it is holds on tighter. I give a hard tug but I get a harder tug back and I'm dragged right into the face of Tony Lejeune.

'Good afternoon,' he says. 'I'm Tony Lejeune. Candidate for Head Boy. Can I rely on your support on Friday?'

'Get off my hand,' I tell him.

But he doesn't get off my hand. Instead he starts shaking it up and down. 'Good to meet you,' he says. 'I'm going to be a listening Head Boy and a leading Head Boy and the people's Head Boy.'

'Get off me,' I tell him.

'What are the issues that most concern you about the school?'

'People breaking other people's hands.'

'That's an issue many people are concerned about and I pledge to do something about it as soon as I'm elected.'

'You could do something about it now.'

'Do you want a sticker or a badge?'

'I want you to let go of my hand.'

'Great. Katie, can we have a sticker over here?' He keeps shaking my hand up and down. 'Believe it, my friend, we can make a difference,' he tells me. 'And a free sticker too. Could Carl Marks offer you that?'

From out of the scrum of kids comes Katie Pierce with a sticker in her hand. That's weird. She normally spends every lunch time smoking non-stop.

'Katie,' Lejeune says. 'Give our newest supporter a sticker.'

'Him?' says Katie Pierce.

'Don't talk about the voters like that,'

snaps Lejeune. 'Some of them have feelings.'

'Tony,' hisses Katie, 'he's not the kind of person we want associated with your campaign. He's not cool or trendy.'

'Isn't he?' says Lejeune.

'No, I've told you to clear it with me before you start putting stickers on people. Look at that girl you gave one to at break. She was fat, Tony. It's totally the wrong image.'

Tony lets go of my hand. 'Sorry, you can't have a sticker,' he tells me. 'But you can vote for me.'

'Thanks a lot,' I tell him sarcastically.

'Don't mention it,' he says, ducking back into the crowd.

'Get lost, Mickey,' says Katie Pierce.

You always think you should hang around after someone's said that to show you're not going to be pushed about. But I've got to be somewhere else so I have to let Katie Pierce think that she can boss me around.

CHAPTER 13

The secretary's office is by the main entrance. There's a window where you can stick your head in to see if she's there. Which she isn't. That's no surprise. All I can see is an empty desk, the register trolley and the TV screens for the new security system. She'll be in the back room smoking and eating chocolates. You catch a glimpse of her sometimes, fag in one hand and hazelnut whirl in the other.

'Hello,' I shout into the empty office.

Nobody comes out of the back room.

'Excuse me,' I shout a bit louder.

Still nobody comes. But I know she's in there. She's really wheezy and she never goes anywhere else. There's this button by the side of the window. It says press for attention. I jam it down. The secretary sticks her head round the door of the back room.

'Miss—' I start.

'Don't press that buzzer!' she snaps. 'That buzzer is for visitors only.'

And then her head disappears again. I

push back down on the buzzer and hold it until her head reappears.

'Miss, it's really important.'

'Take your finger off that buzzer. Do you think the school is made of batteries?'

I'm not taking my finger off anything until she gets herself over here.

'Miss, I need your help.'

'That buzzer!'

'It won't take long, miss.'

The buzzer keeps buzzing. She shakes her head and walks over towards me. When she gets to the window I take my finger away.

'That buzzer is school property. You shouldn't be abusing it.'

'I wasn't abusing it. I was pressing it. That's what buzzers are for.'

'Don't cheek me, young man.'

I could carry on the argument but it's not worth it. She's not the kind of woman who looks like she's open to alternative points of view.

'Miss, I need to find a kid called Alston in Year Eleven. I've got to give him a message from Mr Newman. If he doesn't get it he'll fail all his GCSEs and be taken into care or something. I thought I knew who he was but I got him mixed up with someone else. I need to see his picture. It's really really important.'

I know that what I've said is laying it on a bit thick but I say it fast and make my face look worried while I'm saying it. If you make something sound like it's important and urgent then you can usually make people go for it.

But she doesn't.

'I am not Mr Newman's servant. If the message is so urgent I'm sure he can get it to him himself.'

I made a mistake. Newman's only a teacher. You need more than that to move a secretary.

'Yes, miss. But I can't find him to tell him and I saw Miss Gartree and she said I should come and see you for his picture.'

'Miss Gartree,' she repeats. A deputy head's got her thinking but it hasn't pushed her all the way.

'She was standing next to Mr Walton when she told me and he nodded at what she said.'

That's my last throw unless I tell her that the Prime Minister wants the picture. Is it going to be enough?

She shakes her head. This isn't good. I need to start making progress on this case.

'I suppose if Mr Walton and Miss Gartree suggested it.'

She walks over to the drawer marked Year Eleven and flicks through a couple of files. It doesn't take her long to find Alston and she brings it over. I take a quick glance at the picture. Dorky kid. Really white face. Spots. Side parting. Glasses. Shouldn't be a problem to find. 11C. Tutor room 13.

'I shall point out to Mr Newman that I am a school secretary and not a dogsbody when I see him. Teachers think you've got nothing better to do than rush round after them.'

If she rushed round there'd be an earthquake.

'OK,' I tell her. 'I've got it. Thanks.'

I head off to room 13 and strike lucky as soon as I get there. Even though it's still five minutes before the bell Alston is waiting outside the door. There's nothing sadder than that. Being early for registration. You might as well write a sign on your head saying I HAVE NO FRIENDS AND NOTHING TO DO.

'Hi,' I say. 'Are you Alston?'

'I haven't got any money,' he says straight away.

'I didn't ask you if you've got any money,' I tell him. 'I want to know your name.'

'No money,' he repeats.

Our school is getting out of hand. You can't even ask a kid his name without him thinking you're trying to mug him.

'Look,' I say, 'I don't want your money.'

'I haven't got a mobile,' he adds.

'What?'

'Fifty pence.'

'Hey?'

'A pound. To leave me alone.'

This is stupid. This kid's in Year Eleven. I'm in Year Nine. Where's his self-respect?

'This isn't about money. This is about the school newspaper.'

'What?' he says.

'The school newspaper. You were the editor. Mr Walton sacked you. Why did he sack you, Alston?'

'Why do you want to know?'

It's no use him trying to come the tough guy after he's offered me money just for asking what his name was. I lean in close to him. It's not as effective as it's meant to be because he's taller than me so I end up staring at his chin. I try and make the best of it by putting on my toughest voice. I've been practising it since last weekend. I saw this old black and white film on the TV with a guy whose top lip didn't move. He knew how to talk.

'Because I do. Now tell me and fast. I haven't got much time.'

'What? What?'

'Don't mess me around, Alston.'

'There's nothing to tell. Mr Walton just said he felt that I'd been doing the job for too long and it wasn't fair and someone else deserved a chance.'

'There's more to it than that, Alston. What about the polls?'

'What?'

'Don't come the innocent with me, Alston. Nobody thinks you've done anything wrong . . . yet.'

'I haven't done anything wrong. I don't know about the Poles. I've only ever been to Germany.'

'Not that kind of poll.'

'What kind of pole? The North Pole? The South Pole? I don't know. Penguins?'

'The opinion poll. The one that Walton saw and decided he had to get rid of because he was too frightened of Carl Marks winning the election. That kind of poll.'

'He didn't see that. What are you talking about?'

'Why are you protecting him? What have you got to hide?'

'Me? Nothing. Nothing at all.' He looks away.

'I can see it in your face, Alston. I know there's something. Tell me now because I'll find out anyway.'

'I . . . I . . . I don't know what you're talking about.'

'There's something about that sacking, isn't there, Alston? Something you know. Something that's eating away at your insides. You'll feel better when you tell me.'

'I don't know . . .'

'Yes you do, Alston. What's missing from your story, Alston? What's the truth?'

'The truth?'

'The truth.'

'I . . . I . . . I . . .'

'Get it out.'

'I wasn't sacked. I resigned.'

'You resigned?'

There's one problem with being fourteen and doing a tough voice. Every so often, just when you least need it to, your voice turns into a squeak. Ms Walter says it's puberty but I say it's embarrassing. Whatever it is, it shatters my tough image.

'What did you resign for?'

'Because of her.'

'Who?'

'Nicola Cohen. She's this girl who works on the newspaper.'

I know that but I don't think he needs to know that I know. 'So?'

'So?'

'What did she do?'

'She didn't do anything. It was me.'

'You?'

'I found myself having ... er ... feelings for her. Non-journalistic feelings.'

'Oh.'

I know how that can happen. I've had those feelings myself.

'At first I could keep them hidden but then Mr Walton said that we had to publish every day this week. That meant every afternoon with her. Just the two of us. I would have had to tell her and she'd have rejected me.'

I think he's right there. He's got a side parting and spots.

'So I went to see Mr Walton and said I was resigning. He got all annoyed and said that I was letting the school down in its most important week and that I should carry on. But I said I couldn't. And he said I was a useless lump with no staying power who'd never amount to anything in life.'

That rings true. He's always saying stuff like that to me.

'And then he said that he was going to make this new kid, Sleazer, the editor. Sleazer's just moved over from Australia and it said on his records that he used to run the school paper back in Sydney. I didn't want him to do that because I'd already met Sleazer and I knew that he was a cheap sensationalist who would turn my paper into a comic but Mr Walton said it wasn't any of my business any more and told me to get out of his office. And then, just as I was going, he gave me a black bin bag and told me to fill it with litter from the playground as a punishment for letting him down.'

That sounds like Walton.

'But when I saw Nicola I told her that Walton had sacked me because if I told her I'd resigned she'd have wanted to know why.'

I'm just beginning to realize what everything he's telling me means.

'You mean Walton never knew about the poll?'

'No.'

'And you never got sacked?'

'I've just said that.'

'And Walton wanted you to stay on?'

'Yes.'

That means Walton's in the clear.

Sometimes the truth hurts.

CHAPTER 14

'Do you call that a tree, Mickey?'

I look up. Mr Johns, our drama teacher, is standing over me.

'What?'

'You are supposed to be being a tree.'

I look around me. All the kids in my class are standing up with their arms stretched out. I was thinking about the case so I didn't notice that Johns had finally stopped talking and got us to do something.

'It's about time you concentrated a bit more on your education, Mickey.'

Education. Pretending to be a tree. Education isn't pretending to be a tree. Education is equations and apostrophes and soil erosion in the Nile Delta. Nobody's saying it's any fun but that's what education is. Pretending to be a tree is just a way of making kids look stupid. But he's standing over me so I don't have a choice. I stand up and hold out my arms.

'That's a very limp tree,' says Johns.

'Very dry soil,' I tell him.

'You are a young sapling. Your trunk is slim and strong. Your branches stretch out to the sun.'

I lift my hands up above my head.

'I suppose that will have to do,' says Johns.

He walks off to shout at the morons at the back who have tangled all their legs together and are claiming to be a big bush. They think that's very funny.

I keep my hands in the air and get back to thinking about the case. Have I been too quick to let Walton off the hook? Maybe Alston didn't tell me the truth. He looked like he was telling the truth but he gave in so easily. He was almost too weak, too eager to tell me what I wanted to know. Maybe Walton had threatened him with expulsion if he told the truth.

'Class!' Mr Johns claps his hands. 'Close your eyes.'

I don't close my eyes completely. I've been at this school nearly three years and one thing I've learnt is that you never close your eyes.

'Now,' says Johns. 'You are all trees. Together you are a forest. A rain forest in South America. Feel the humidity. You are hot, hot, hot.'

There's no chance of that in our school. Walton switches the heating off in January.

'The wind rushes through the trees. What sound does it make?'

Someone makes a big farting noise. The class start laughing.

'Quiet!' shouts Johns. 'Anybody laughing will be put in detention.'

The class quietens down.

'The trees sway in the breeze. They sway in the breeze. They sway in the— oh, forget it – the wind has dropped. There is a sound.'

Someone makes another farting noise.

'Be quiet!' shouts Johns. 'It is the sound of a chain saw. The loggers are coming through the forest, sawing down the trees. The trees that have been there for hundreds of years. But in seconds the loggers chop them down. You feel the pain as the chain saw cuts through your bark but you cannot scream. And now you are falling, falling, falling . . .'

'Ow.'

I open my eyes fully. The Thick Girl with Glasses is lying on the floor.

Johns rushes over to her. 'Are you all right?' he shouts.

She sits up. There's blood coming out of the side of her head. Everywhere I go today girls are having accidents. I get as far from her as possible. I don't want Walton coming up with a pattern and accusing me of being a serial killer.

'You said fall, sir,' explains the Thick Girl with Glasses.

'It was a metaphor,' shouts Johns. 'You're not really a tree.'

I'd have an argument with him on that one.

'But I felt like a tree, sir,' says the Thick Girl with Glasses. 'Does this mean I get a credit?'

'Yes,' says Johns. 'Definitely.'

'Two credits?'

'Well . . .'

'I feel dizzy.'

'Two credits.'

Johns tells us all to pack our stuff up and he takes her off to the medical room. The morons at the back do what they always do when they're left alone in a classroom, which is to start breaking things. Katie Pierce and her gang go outside to make calls on their mobiles. They only get them out so often to show off. They probably ring each other even though they're standing side by side. You hear people on mobile phones and they are always saying the dumbest things in really loud voices. Mobile phones are just an excuse for boring people to ram their tedious lives right in your face.

Umair comes up to me.

'All right?' I say.

'Why did you pull my chair out in English?'

He looks angry. I'd forgotten I haven't got round to saying sorry or anything.

'Oh,' I say. 'It's this thing I'm doing at the moment. I didn't mean it against you.'

'What thing?' he asks.

I don't say anything right away. We used to be mates and if we still were then I'd let him in on it. But I don't know. I'm still deciding when he makes up my mind for me.

'Forget it,' he says. 'You're getting weird, you know. Sad.' And he walks off.

I can't believe it. He's calling me sad. He goes to chess club.

I still feel bad though.

The bell goes before Johns gets back and so we all walk off. This has been one of the longest days I remember and all I want to do is get back to my shed, have a packet of crisps and a Coke and relax but I can't. I've got one more thing to clear up before I can call it a day.

And it's still the opinion poll.

Nicola Cohen did it first. It showed 55% to 45% for Tony Lejeune. Alston was going to print it. Then he resigned. Kelvin Sleazer got the job. When the poll appeared it showed 100% to Lejeune and 0% to Carl Marks. Kelvin Sleazer has to know where the new poll came from. I head off to the school newspaper office, hoping he's still there.

He is. I knock on the door and walk in.

'What do you want, mate?'

'A bit of help, mate,' I shoot back. I figure I'll try talking like him in order to put him at his ease.

'I'm busy, mate.'

'Be a mate, mate.'

You just finish off with 'mate' every time you stop talking. It's not hard.

'Make it quick, mate.'

'Is that tomorrow's paper, mate?' I see it lying on the desk. I want to get his confidence before I start on the stuff I really want to know.

'Yeah, mate. I've got to do this Head Boy stuff on the front page because Walton says it's a matter of public interest. Do you know what that means, mate?'

I shake my head. Never make someone

you want a favour from feel like they're stupider than you. And anyway, I don't know.

'But page two's where we get the Sleazer sensations starting. Look at this.'

I look at what he shows me. On page two there are pictures of four girls and underneath it says: 'Win a date with your favourite Year 11 babe.'

He sees me looking.

'I wanted them topless,' he explains. 'But Walton said they looked better in school uniform. What do you think, mate?'

'Great,' I tell him, looking a bit closer. And then suddenly I don't think it's great at all. One of the girls is my sister.

'What's the matter, mate?' he says.

'Er . . . nothing,' I tell him, trying to make my voice sound casual. 'How did you get the girls to agree to it? They might end up having to go out with a Year Seven boy with a snotty nose.'

'Oh, that's easy, mate. You just tell them that they're really thin and pretty and they're all going to be models and that this is really good publicity. Tell girls anything, mate. It doesn't matter what they think. It's what they look like that matters.'

That would have worked with my sister. She wants to be a model more than anything else in the world. She never eats anything but salads and she puts this stuff on her face at night to make her skin stay young even though she's only sixteen.

It's strange. I can be as horrible as I like to my sister and say really nasty stuff to her and she can to me. But when other people say the same stuff or try to make a fool of her then it's up to me to try and stop it. It might not make much sense but that's the brother-and-sister code and there's no getting away from it. And when I think of this scumbag lying to her so he can put her picture in the school newspaper I feel really angry. What I'd like to do right now is give him a good smack on the jaw and tear his newspaper up in front of him. But I can't. First, I need his help and, second, he's bigger than me. So I don't say anything.

'We're going to have loads more babes in the next issue once this stupid election is over,' he tells me. 'But you're going to have to push off now, mate, because I've got an interview with Tony Lejeune which is going on the front page tomorrow.'

'Right,' I say. 'One thing before I go, mate.

I talked to Nicola Cohen about the opinion poll and she said that her poll was fifty-five per cent to forty-five per cent in favour of Tony Lejeune. But when it came out it said a hundred per cent to Lejeune and nought per cent to Marks. What happened to the first poll?'

'There were mistakes in it, mate. The figures got confused with the Head Girl's poll or something. It had to be changed.'

Now we're getting somewhere.

'Who decided to change it?' I ask. 'You?'

'No, mate. I had nothing to do with it.'

'Walton?'

'Walton? He only interferes when I want to put topless girls in.'

I'm getting lost. 'Well, who then?' I ask.

'The only person who could have known that she'd made a mistake in the first poll, mate.'

I don't get where he's going. He looks at me like I'm thick.

'Jeez, mate. Do I need to spell it out for you? The person who changed the poll was Nicola Cohen.'

CHAPTER 15

I take a long swig of Coke and stick a hand-ful of salt 'n' vinegar into my mouth. I haven't been this confused since Mr Barlow told us about quadratic equations. Nicola Cohen changed the poll. If she changed the poll why did she tell me about the original poll? If she didn't change the poll why did Sleazer tell me that she did? I mean, I wouldn't trust him with my sister but he's got no reason to lie about Nicola Cohen. And he looked like he was telling the truth. But then so did Nicola Cohen. Someone's got to be lying, haven't they? But which one?

There's a knock at the shed door.

'Yeah,' I say.

It opens. It's Carl Marks. Just what I need. A client when I've got nothing to tell him apart from the fact that I'm very confused. Which I don't think is the information he's paying for.

'Hello,' he says. 'Do you mind if I sit down?'

I nod towards the box. He sits down. He smiles at me.

'I came to tell you that you were right,' he says.

This is a rare experience. People don't usually associate me with the word 'right'.

'I spoke to my friends and, do you know, they were a little embarrassed by my wanting to be Head Boy. And my History teacher had got my paper mixed up with another pupil's and in fact I did get an A. So you see, it's rather embarrassing, but you were right all along. There never was anything going on. So, of course, you won't have found anything out. We can call it all off now. Of course, I'll pay you for today and then—'

'What about the posters?' I throw in.

'Well, you said it yourself. People are always ripping them down. I was just being paranoid.'

'No, you weren't,' I tell him.

'I beg your pardon?'

'There is something going on.'

'What is it?'

He's paying the bills so I tell him. I try to make it as clear as possible but somehow it ends up sounding muddled anyway. When I finish he doesn't look impressed.

'I owe you an apology,' he tells me. 'I've transferred my paranoia to you but you have a more extreme form.'

'I don't,' I tell him. 'There's something going on but I just don't know what it is yet. You've got to give me some more time. Look at that poll. A hundred per cent for Lejeune, nothing for you. Don't you think that's a bit weird?'

'Oh, I don't think we should pay too much attention to opinion polls,' he says. 'It's what the people do in the ballot box that matters.'

'But—'

'And my campaign didn't really start until today at the hustings. I thought I won over a few supporters there.'

It seems a long time ago but I can still remember the hustings better than that.

'How come your posters get ripped down and his don't?'

'There's bound to be a logical explanation for it.'

'What is it?'

'Coincidence.'

'Look, you asked me to look into this and I'm telling you there's something that stinks but I'm not sure what it is yet. You've got to trust me on that.'

I shouldn't have said that. I sounded all wrong. Like I was begging him to believe me. Once you start begging people to believe you they never do.

He stands up, pulls some money out of his pocket and puts it on the desk. 'I appreciate all you've done,' he says, 'but I really think that everything is OK with this election. I'm prepared to fight it on the issues and I'm sure I'll get a fair hearing. We must await the verdict of the electorate.' And he nods to me and walks out.

I've lost my client. The case is finished.

I'm in a bad mood when I get into the house for tea. My sister's already at the table. She's reading the problem page in some stupid magazine. All they are is girls writing letters asking whether they should have sex with their boyfriends or not. It seems so dumb to me. Why would you take the advice of some stranger who's never met you or your boyfriend? Why not make up your own mind?

I'm still mad about losing the case so I decide to offer these ideas to Karen.

'You're so immature,' she says without looking up.

'Not like you,' I shoot back. ' "Win a date with a Year Eleven babe".'

She looks up this time. 'How did you know about that?' she says. 'It doesn't come out until tomorrow.'

'I know, right? It's pathetic.'

'No, it's not. Kelvin says it will raise my profile, which is essential if I'm to become a model.'

That's my sister's answer to everything. She wants to be a model so anything she thinks might help is OK.

'It's cheap,' I tell her. 'You shouldn't let yourself be a prize.'

'I'm not a prize.' She looks really angry. 'Kelvin says that I just have to have lunch with the boy in the school canteen. That's all.'

'Kelvin's a scumbag,' I tell her. 'If he could have got it past Walton, he'd have tried to make you go topless.'

'Kelvin discussed that with me,' she says. 'He told me that any shots would be very artistic. He's very interested in my career.'

I laugh.

'Mickey, not all boys are lowlifes like you. Don't judge everyone by your own dirty mind.'

Kelvin Sleazer talked to her about topless photos but I'm the one with a dirty mind.

'Karen,' I try, 'you don't need to do this.'

'Grow up, Mickey. I want to do it. It's my body and it's my life. Just accept it and move on.'

She's always talking like she's on an American chat show. She thinks it makes her sophisticated. I hear someone coming downstairs.

'Does Dad know you're a prize in the school newspaper?'

She looks worried for the first time. I don't think she's too confident that my dad is just going to accept it and move on. He's more likely to choke on his dinner and yell his head off.

'Are you going to tell him?'

'Tell me what?'

My dad walks into the room. I look at Karen and then I look at my dad. If I told him he'd stop it but it would be nasty and my family can do without nasty at the moment. My dad goes mad about everything, my mum hardly talks at all any more and me and Karen are either out or in our rooms. We only ever see each other at tea time and we try our best to ignore each other then. It's the only way we get along without shouting. The other thing is that if you grass your sister up you never know what could get thrown back at you. And then there's the rules. However much you hate your sister you're supposed to be on the same side as her when it comes to your parents. It's another bit of the brother-and-sister code.

'Tell me what?' repeats my dad.

I look at Karen. 'Nothing,' I tell my dad.

I've lost my case, a girl who I really like thinks I'm a moron and my sister is a prize in the school newspaper. Not exactly a great day.

CHAPTER 16

I always told myself when I decided to be a detective that I was going to do it properly. And what properly meant was being paid. So if a client decided that he didn't want to go ahead with the investigation then I dropped it and I walked away. That way you know you're being professional. If you just look into something for the hell of it you're like those dopey posh kids and their dog who are always going round having adventures and drinking ginger beer all the time. I read those books before I knew any better and I always wanted the baddies to get away with it and the ginger beer to be poisoned. I said that to my mum when I was little and she gave me this really weird look and made me an appointment at the doctor's. He told her to keep a close eye on me and come back immediately if I started being cruel to animals. I was never allowed to clean out the hamster's cage unsupervised again.

But it's easy to make rules. It's a bit

different when you're pulled off the case when there are a lot of things you don't know and you want a few answers.

My bike's got a puncture so I'm walking to school. I'm still trying to decide whether to carry on with the case when something happens that makes up my mind for me. I go through the back gate and start to cut across the school field. There's this little grassy hill near the gate. It's been there ever since I came to Hanford High and I've never paid it any attention, which has never done me any harm up to now. But today I should have given it a closer look because then I might have had some warning. Because it's from behind there that they come.

I feel a big bang in my back and I'm knocked forward. I try to keep my balance but the force of the hit is too much. I smash into the ground.

'Get him.'

One body lands on top of me. Then another. Someone rams my head down and I get a big mouthful of mud and grass. Then someone else jumps on my legs. I jam my head up to try to yell but instead I just start coughing. Whoever is behind my head rams it back into the ground.

'Shut up.'

'Yeah. Shut up.'

'He'd better shut up.'

I haven't said anything but as they're all so convinced that I have I might as well give it a go.

'Hey,' I say.

'*Shut up!*' they all say at once.

I suppose I should have expected that.

'Are you Mickey Sharp?'

Up to now I just thought it was some jerks jumping on my head. This is always happening in my school. They jump on your head for a while and then they get off and go away. But these guys don't want to jump on just anyone's head. They want to jump on mine.

'Oi, did you hear me? Are you Mickey Sharp?'

'No,' I say into the ground.

'What?'

'No, I'm not.'

'Oh.'

'He's not Mickey Sharp.'

'I thought he was.'

'Well, he doesn't think he is.'

'What do we do now?'

'Check his bag.'

The weight on my legs disappears. This could get nasty.

'He is Mickey Sharp.'

My head's yanked back out of the grass by the hair.

'You *are* Mickey Sharp.'

'I know,' I say.

'Why did you say you weren't?'

'I think I got temporary amnesia when you hit me on the head. It's all coming back to me now. If you stopped hitting me I'd be far more helpful.'

'Don't tell me not to hit you.'

'I wasn't telling, I was just suggesting.'

Bang. He clouts me again.

'Now listen up. We've got a message for you.'

'I'm doing my best. But you keep distracting me with violence.'

'Right then. This is the message. It's "Don't ..."' And then he stops.

'Don't what?' I'm trying to help.

'Don't rush me.'

'What does that mean?' I say.

'Shut up.'

And just for a change he slams my head into the ground.

'Can anybody remember the message?

140

I've forgotten it.'

'I thought you knew it.'

'It was something to do with the Head Boy.'

'Oh yeah.'

'No, no, I remember it. She said, "Tell him to keep out of the Head Boy election or it will be the worse for him." '

'That was it.'

'Yeah, that was it.'

'What does "the worse for him" mean?'

'Shut up. I don't know.'

My head gets yanked back again.

'Listen, Sharp.' He tells me the message again. 'You got that, Sharp?'

'Yeah,' I tell them.

'OK. Now stick your face in the ground and count to a hundred. Don't look round until you've got there. You understand?'

I tell them I understand. It's not a difficult concept.

They get off me. I keep my face in the ground a few seconds but no way am I going to count to a hundred. They're going to be running away and I want to see who they are. I turn round. The Psychos are standing right behind me.

'We told you to count to a hundred,' says one of them.

'I'm a fast counter,' I tell them.

They move towards me.

'It's a gift,' I add.

They keep coming.

CHAPTER 17

I look into the mirror in the boys' toilet to see if I've got the blood off. The mirror's all shattered so you can't get a decent look at yourself but I seem to have got rid of it. I head off to class. But I don't get there.

'Sharp.'

It's Walton. I've heard about these celebrities who have stalkers – these people who follow them everywhere because they're obsessed with them. I figure Walton must be mine.

'Come here.'

I go over.

'Walk, lad. Don't slouch.'

I hate that. Teachers think they can tell you everything. I keep slouching along just to wind him up.

'Look at yourself, lad. Is this any way to come to school?'

I look at myself. I'm a bit muddy. 'I fell over,' I tell him.

'You know why you fell over, don't you, lad?'

I shake my head.

'Because you don't walk properly. There's no pride in your step. You drag your feet.'

I feel like telling him he might drag his feet if he'd been beaten up that morning for nothing but I don't. He wouldn't believe me anyway and it would just lead to trouble.

'Now get to class. You're late.'

I turn round and head off to my form room. I know he's watching me so I make sure I walk extra slowly and that my feet drag right along the ground. I have to put up with lessons and homework and my dad so I don't see why he shouldn't be prepared to put up with me walking the way I want to.

I get into class and things get even better. Newman gives me a late detention and the morons at the back see that I'm all muddy and rip out a big chorus of 'Mickey is a tramp'. Newman shuts them up eventually but not before they've managed to say it about a hundred times. That's the trouble with the morons. They don't come up with many sentences so when they get a new one they really work it to death.

'I've got something you need to see, Mickey.'

Katie Pierce is standing in front of me. She pulls a copy of the school newspaper from her bag and flattens it out on my desk. There's an opened envelope inside it. It's got 'Kelvin Sleazer, Editor, School Newspaper' written on it in really neat handwriting.

'What's that?' I say.

'Nothing.' Katie scoops it up quickly and points to the article in the paper. 'That's your sister, isn't it, Mickey?'

A picture of Karen stares up at me. And the line WIN A DATE WITH YOUR FAVOURITE YEAR 11 BABE.

'So?' I try to look like it's no big deal. It's not too hard to pull off because I already knew about it.

'It's a shame she can't find dates the normal way – you know, by having boys ask her.'

'Thanks for your concern,' I tell her.

'Don't mention it,' she says. 'I hate to see a girl so desperate that she's got to advertise. Today it's the paper. Tomorrow it could be a telephone box.'

'Forget it,' I tell her.

'But I can't forget it. We girls have got to

145

stick together. We're like one big sisterhood. I'm going to help her out.'

'I don't—'

'Don't thank me,' she says. 'Just look behind you.'

I turn round. The morons at the back have each got a copy of the school newspaper in front of them. They're filling out their names on the form.

'They didn't know the answer to the question that might win them a date with your sister,' Katie explained, 'so I helped them out. Like I said, don't thank me.'

And she walks off. The morons at the back on a date with my sister! I'd be humiliated. I don't even want to think about it. She's left the paper on my desk. I flick it over to get Karen's face out of sight and see the front-page headline: TONY LEJEUNE – HANFORD'S NEXT HEAD BOY!

There's nothing like unbiased reporting. The election isn't until tomorrow and they're already calling him the next Head Boy. I skim over the article. It's just says Tony Lejeune is wonderful in about twenty different ways. But at the bottom of the page is a little story that really gets my attention.

Sources close to Carl Marks (outsider in the Head Boy race) have told this reporter that, distraught at his appalling opinion poll ratings, he is considering withdrawing from the election. One person close to the campaign said, 'Marks knows he's not the best man. He may even vote for Lejeune himself.'

But it's not the story that really gets me thinking. It's what it says at the bottom –

by Nicola Cohen

She's still writing for the newspaper. And it's really anti-Marks stuff she's putting out too. After all that stuff she told me about being sacked. And then something else clicks in my mind. When The Psychos were sitting on top of me trying to remember the message they let something slip. They said 'she said' about the person who gave them the message. It didn't register right off because you don't concentrate your best when you've got your face full of grass and three big lumps are sitting on your back. But who can the 'she' be? Who's the only girl who knows that I'm working on the Head Boy case? Nicola Cohen. Did she get The Psychos to beat me up? What about the day before when The Psychos gave me grief? Who arranged the meeting place and wasn't there in time, giving The Psychos a good chance to check out what I looked like, even though as it turned out they were too dumb to remember? Could it be that she's been playing me all this time? I thought she was such a cool girl. I must be a terrible judge of character.

So that's everything. She knows exactly what I've got. She's probably told Tony Lejeune. This is one big zero of a result. My first big failure. Outwitted and out-thought.

I check behind me. The morons at the back are still filling out the form in the school newspaper. It's only a short form but writing isn't their strong point. They usually use pens for sticking in each other so the fact that you can get ink out of them probably comes as a shock. Maybe I can do something about them.

CHAPTER 18

'Did I tell you to print? Did I? No. But you pressed print anyway. How many times did you press print?'

'About a hundred, sir. I thought it was bust.'

'And pressing print a hundred times is going to make it better, is it?'

'Don't know.'

'You don't know? Everybody get away from their keyboards. I don't want to see anybody touching a single key until the technician gets here to sort this out.'

It's hard to concentrate on the case when there's a teacher shouting down your ear. Not that he's shouting at me for a change. He's shouting at the Thick Girl with Glasses but she's at the computer next to me and so the shouting still goes in my ear. It's a bit like passive smoking only noisier.

Our IT lessons are always the same. We sit down at the computers. Mr Lynch tells us to do something. We start off doing it. Someone does something stupid and the network goes down and then we spend the rest of the lesson with Mr Lynch shouting at us and stopping anybody touching a computer. Well, if we're lucky he shouts at us. If we're unlucky he spends the rest of the time telling us about last night's episode of *Star Trek*.

'Are you touching that computer?'

'What?'

This time it *is* me he's after. I'd forgotten to move my hands away.

'You are touching that computer. Get your hands away from it. That's an expensive piece of equipment.'

I put my hands in my pockets.

'Get your hands out of your pockets.'

I take my hands out of my pockets and show them to him. 'What do you want me to do with them?' I ask.

He looks like he's about to explode all over me but then luckily one of the morons at the back shouts out something rude as a suggestion and he gets distracted and goes over to shout at him.

IT is proof that whenever you give something even half decent to teachers they'll make it boring. Computers are good for one thing and that's playing games on. That's what they were invented for. Everybody in the world knows that apart from IT teachers. They think computers are good because you can do spreadsheets and databases on them and you can make your work look like a real newspaper. It's just another bit of proof that teachers aren't like other human beings.

Still, now I don't need to pretend to work I can think about the case properly. I know that Nicola Cohen is involved in all the stuff that's been going on but I still don't know why. There must be a reason why she's doing what she's doing. There must be some connection with Lejeune. Maybe she fancies him or maybe they're secretly going out together. But I need to get some proof. I need to see them together. So I'm going to have to follow one of them until they meet up. I can't follow Nicola – she knows me too well. I'm going to have to go after Lejeune. The problem with going after Lejeune is that this morning I had The Psychos sitting on my head telling me not to. I need some way to keep them off my back as well as my head. I know they like fags. Maybe if I've got a few when I next see them it could buy me some time.

'Sharp.'

I'm dragged back to the real world by Lynch's voice.

'Are you listening, Sharp?'

'Yes,' I say. This is always the right answer to that question.

'What have I been saying?'

'Oh,' I say. This is always the wrong answer to that question.

'Come on, Sharp. Why should Captain Kirk have expected Klingon involvement when Mr Spock's sensor went dead immediately after they beamed down to the desert planet of Andromeda Nine?'

I shake my head.

'You'd know if you'd been listening, Sharp.'

'Sir?' I ask him.

'Yes, Sharp?'

'Do you think you might need help?'

You could tell he wanted to give me a detention but, mad as he is, even he can see that he's on dodgy ground and so he has to be content with telling me to 'boldly go out of his sight' when the bell goes. I think it might have been a joke. You never know with teachers.

Still, I've got better things to do than worry about Mr Lynch's mental health.

You're not supposed to go out during break but the teacher who's supposed to be watching the front gate hasn't turned up on his break duty yet so I've got a clear run. I head over to the paper shop.

'Oi. You. Get out.'

I look up. The owner is staring at me.

'What've I done?'

'Two at a time. You're the third. Get out.'

I've got no option. I get out of his stupid shop and wait outside until one of the other kids comes out. Luckily, it doesn't take too long. I get back in fast and go up to the counter.

'Can I have some cigarettes?' I ask quietly.

'How many?'

'Three,' I tell him. I need one for each of The Psychos.

'Ten or twenty?' he shoots back.

'Oh, I meant ten.' I knew they didn't come in threes but I wasn't thinking.

'What kind?'

'Don't mind.'

'What?'

'Any cigarettes.'

'Are you winding me up?'

I shake my head. How difficult can it be? All I want is ten cigarettes. 'Them,' I say, pointing at a packet behind his head. 'The gold ones.'

But he doesn't turn round. Instead he leans over the counter, grabs my coat and pulls me right across it.

'Get off!' I shout. I'd heard that cigarettes killed you but I didn't think that meant the guy you buy them off did it personally.

He stops pulling when I'm lying across the counter.

'Help,' I shout.

He holds my head down with one hand and pulls my shirt up with the other. My mind goes blank and my body goes limp. Is he going to kill me?

And then before I know it, I'm back on the right side of the counter again and he's staring at me as though nothing has happened. 'You're clean,' he tells me.

'What?' I say.

'Clean.'

'Did my mum ask you to check?' I ask him but he doesn't get it.

'I don't know your mother, son. But I do know that the TV people have been sending kids under sixteen in with hidden cameras on them to buy cigarettes and then naming and shaming on the local news. I couldn't have that happen to me. I've got a business to run.'

He gets the cigarettes down. I give him the money.

'Hey,' I say once I've got the fags safely in my pocket. 'Why don't you just stop selling fags to kids under sixteen? Then you wouldn't need to worry about the TV people.'

He looks at me like I'm mad. 'Kid,' he says, 'I've got two children of my own. You think I want them to go to that excuse of a school that you go to? Let me tell you that I don't. I've been here fifteen years. All the kids at your school are foul-mouthed and dis-respectful. I want better for my children so I send them to a private school. You think it's cheap? It's not. It's very expensive. The only way I can afford to keep my children at private school is if at least half the kids in your school smoke. So offer yours around, all right?'

There are some people about who are just too mad and you need to get away from them fast.

Standing outside the shop is Carl Marks. 'Did you know Year Nines aren't allowed out at lunch time?' he asks.

'Thanks for telling me.'

'If I were Head Boy that would change. All pupils would have freedom of movement. It's a guaranteed right within the European Union. Did you know that?'

'Er . . . no,' I say.

'Mr Walton may be in breach of European law. We could take a case to Brussels. Or is it Strasbourg?'

'I don't know,' I tell him.

'I plan to liberate the entire lower school. The fences round the school are like the Berlin Wall and they—'

I cut him short. 'What do you want?'

'Oh yes,' he says, 'I almost forgot. I need you back on the case.'

'You've only just taken me off the case,' I point out. I don't think I need to mention that I'm working on it anyway.

'Something's come up. The situation's changed.'

'What?'

'Someone's come to see me. They've convinced me that there's something bad happening.'

'Who?'

'It doesn't matter. Some girl called Cohen.'

'Nicola Cohen?'

'Yes. Do you know her?'

I shake my head. And I'm not lying. I may have met Nicola Cohen but I'm becoming surer and surer that I don't really know her.

'Anyway, I need you back on the case, right now.'

'That'll be seven pounds a day plus expenses,' I tell him. I figure that he agreed to my price so quickly last time that I might as well see if he'll agree to a little bit more.

'Seven pounds?' he says. 'It was six yesterday.'

'Inflation,' I tell him, shaking my head and looking sorry. 'What can I say?'

'You're taking advantage of me,' Carl says.

I shrug my shoulders.

'I haven't got any choice,' he tells me. 'Seven pounds a day it is. But you'd better be worth it.'

He walks off. I'm back on the case. Now for Lejeune.

CHAPTER 19

He isn't that hard to find. I suppose if you're standing in an election it's a good idea to go somewhere where people can see you. Lejeune and his team are standing next to the lunch queue. I recognize Katie Pierce and Julie Reece with him. There are some other girls but I don't know who they are. The lunch queue goes right down the corridor outside the hall and they're wandering up and down asking kids if they'll vote for him. I make myself inconspicuous by standing in the queue but I keep letting other kids past me so that I don't end up at the front and have to get some food. A couple of kids look at me weirdly but most of them are too pleased to get past. Lunch is the best bit of most kids' days at school. It shows what terrible places schools are when the only thing to look forward to is cold chips and custard with skin on.

The good thing is that Lejeune and his team don't seem to be having that much success. When I got caught up in his campaigning yesterday I got the idea that he was doing all right but I didn't really hang around to check it out properly. Now with a bit more time I can see that nobody really looks that interested. The kids just don't seem to want to know him. Which at least proves that the kids at my school have got a little bit of sense. And that's not something I admit all that often.

As Lejeune gets down the line towards me I figure I'd better get myself out of the way because Katie Pierce is following right behind him and I don't want her seeing me. So, when he's about three kids away I bend down to do up my shoelace. This is a pretty brave thing to do in the lunch queue because, if you get your head down in the same place as other people's feet, there's a good chance that you're going to get it kicked. Too many kids in my school don't like to miss the opportunity of casual violence against a stranger.

Luckily though I don't attract any boots in the face and I can still hear what's going on.

'Would you like to vote for me?' That's Lejeune's voice. All smooth and pretend friendly.

'No.' That's the kid in front of me. All rough and get out of my face.

'For Head Boy. I'll be very good. I'll make this school a people's school.' Lejeune again. Still cool and calm.

'I hate people.' The kid in front of me again. Still tough and possibly psychotic.

'Oh. What do you like?' Lejeune's less cool this time.

'Bull terriers. Do you reckon you could make it so that we could have them in lessons?' The kid in front of me suddenly sounds interested.

'Er . . . I'm not sure. I'll look into it. I'll get back to you.'

The queue moves forward and the bull terrier fan moves on. Kids shove past me and clamber over me, the smell of burger and chips leaking out of the canteen making them whimper and salivate. I can't hear Lejeune's voice. He must have moved down the queue again. Unfortunately with a crush all around me I'm in no position to follow him.

Kids don't queue like adults queue. You see adults in a queue like in the supermarket or waiting for a bus and they shuffle forward and then they stop for a bit and then they shuffle forward a bit more and everyone stays on their feet. Kids don't queue like that. They're fine when the queue has stopped but as soon as it starts to move they all get the idea that it's not going to stop again and they're going to get right to the front without another wait. Unfortunately, whoever is at the front of the queue doesn't know this and when they stop the next person stops but the kids behind him don't. They keep on moving and then pushing and then heaving and there's only one way it's all going to end. And that's with the dinner ladies at our school going on strike until Walton agrees to pay them danger money. One of them has to wear a neck brace permanently ever since the day the rumour went down the line that the chips had run out and there was a stampede.

The problem with the queue is rammed home to me as I'm the only kid in the whole thing that isn't moving. As kids go past me, round me and over me I get banged, shoved, kicked and trodden on. I bet Carl Marks doesn't realize the trouble I'm going to for him.

'This is a disaster.'

My feelings exactly but they're not my

words. It's Tony Lejeune's voice. He must have come back down the queue towards me.

'Calm down, Tony. It doesn't matter.'

And that's Katie Pierce. They're near me but they can't see me because I'm underneath what feels like a rugby scrum.

'Doesn't matter? We need to do better. All they care about is food and pit bull terriers.'

'Tony, how many times? It doesn't matter what *is* going on. It matters what people *think* is going on. All we need are a couple more good headlines in the school paper and everyone will be so sure that everyone else is going to vote for you that they'll all vote for you too. Kids are like sheep.'

Katie Pierce doesn't seem to have too much respect for the voters. The trouble is that for once I agree with her. Most kids don't like standing out from the crowd because one step away from standing out from the crowd is getting beaten up by the crowd. So they do what they think everybody else is doing.

'What do we do? Use Nicola Cohen?'

I was right. Nicola Cohen was working for his team all the time.

'No, I've got other things planned for

Nicola. I'll tell you about it in the strategy meeting in room nineteen after school,' says Katie. 'We'll get our next good headline another way.'

Even though I'm proved right about Nicola Cohen a bit of me still wishes I wasn't. There aren't many kids in this world that are all right and when you find one it isn't a good feeling to discover they've been selling you a line the whole time. Especially when you started off by buying it.

'How?' asks Lejeune.

'Trust me, Tony.'

I'm still crouched down but I flick a glance around some kid's leg and see they've turned away. Finally I'm able to stand up. I keep myself pressed right against the wall of the corridor. Luckily the kid standing next to me is a fat one so I can keep out of sight and just look round him to see what's going on. Katie Pierce is on her phone. At first I can't hear what she's saying but then whoever it is on the other end is stupid enough to argue with her and she starts shouting.

'I'm telling you there is something happening that you need to see ... I don't care if you are in a meeting ... I don't care if you are talking to the hottest babe in Year

Eleven ... There is a major news story breaking and you need to be here to cover it ... What are my qualifications to tell if something is a great story? I'll tell you what they are. My mum's a school governor and if you don't get up here in two minutes she'll be on the phone to Mr Walton complaining that your newspaper is a sexist tabloid rag and you won't be editor tomorrow morning ... I'll see you in two minutes.'

She snaps shut her phone and turns round to Lejeune and Julie Reece and smiles. 'Julie, you'd better go. He's coming.'

Julie Reece walks off down the corridor. I suppose she's going to give Sleazer an escort to make sure he doesn't change his mind. Except that she's going the opposite way to the newspaper office.

'Great,' snaps back Lejeune. 'He's coming and frankly, Katie, there's nothing to see apart from voters ignoring me and thinking about food. That's not the kind of coverage I need.'

'Relax, Tony,' says Katie. 'There'll be something for him to see. Don't I always make sure that there's something for people to see?'

'But two minutes ...'

Katie turns away from him, puts two fingers into her mouth and blows. The noise is astonishing. I didn't think girls could whistle like that. The effect is instant. Everybody in the queue shuts up.

'Hi, everybody.' She's got this big friendly smile on her face and a bunch of paper in her hand which she holds up in the air. 'Anybody fancy a free lunch? I've got a whole load of dinner tickets here. If you want one all you need to do is start chanting, "Tony! Tony!" when I do and keep going for thirty seconds. All right?'

Dinner tickets are like a school's second currency after money. Poor kids get given five at the start of the week and then they get free lunches. Except that the kid who's meant to get the lunch almost never does. Instead, as soon as they've got them they sell them. A dinner ticket is worth about a quid in our school canteen but on a Monday morning they sell for about forty pence each. A bunch of five goes for two quid. It doesn't seem to make sense at first – selling something worth five quid for two quid – until you realize that two quid is almost exactly the cost of ten cigarettes. In the end it all comes back to fags. I'm not too worried though because I don't figure that this is going to come off. Kate is trying to buy publicity but kids aren't going to chant, 'Tony! Tony!' just for a dinner ticket.

'Tony!' she starts.

Nothing happens.

'Tony! Tony!'

Still nothing. I lean back against the corridor wall. We all have favourite ways of spending our lunch time and watching Katie Pierce make a fool of herself ranks high on mine.

'Tony! Tony!'

She's still on her own. Her voice sounds really pathetic. I wonder how long it'll take before she gives up. As far as I'm concerned this can go on until the end of the day. Into the corridor, notebook in hand, comes Kelvin Sleazer. This is getting better.

There's one thing about soaps that are true to life. As soon as you start relaxing and enjoying yourself something comes along and wrecks it. And when Kelvin Sleazer is two steps into the corridor along it comes.

'Tony! Tony! Tony!'

They start chanting. Katie drops out before Sleazer sees her and points to the crowd. He starts making notes in his notebook.

'Tony! Tony! Tony!'

They're getting louder. This is terrible. For a second I think that Katie has drugged them all so that they do what she says but then the real reason clicks in.

Year Sevens.

I hadn't noticed because I was so busy concentrating on what was going on between Katie and Lejeune. But it's gone quarter to one. That's the time when only Year Sevens are allowed to go in for lunch. The rule was brought in last year because when everybody could queue up at any time only one or two Year Sevens were actually getting to the front without having their lunch money nicked. It was like one of those nature documentaries that Mr Crick showed us in Science so he could get on with his marking where you'd got these seals paddling across this little bay and you'd got these killer whales swimming nearby. Not many seals made it. So, to give the seals more chance they banned all other year groups from the lunch queue until one o'clock.

'Tony! Tony! Tony!'

Lejeune's trying to look modest but he just looks creepy. It doesn't matter too much though because Sleazer's writing like crazy in his notebook. I've got to hand it to Katie. She really pulled this one off. If she'd had a load of Year Nine and Ten kids she'd have got nowhere. Their credibility is worth more than a dinner ticket but Year Sevens haven't got any credibility to lose. They wear full school uniform and still get excited when they get credits. They'll do anything.

'Tony! Tony! Tony!'

'What is the meaning of this?'

It's Walton.

The Year Sevens shut up. Katie Pierce makes some kind of sign to Tony Lejeune and he starts to edge down the corridor away from Walton. Kelvin Sleazer follows him. Walton starts walking along the queue yelling the whole time.

'This is a school not a football ground. How dare you make so much noise? One more sound out of this queue and nobody will get any lunch at all.'

You can tell Walton's enjoying himself. He loves shouting at kids.

'Does everybody understand that? Has anybody got a problem with that?'

There's silence in the corridor. Walton looks up and down the queue with this smug grin on his face. But then his grin disappears because one little Year Seven kid has put his hand up.

'*What?*' barks Walton.

'Sir,' pipes up this little kid, 'when are we going to get our free dinner tickets?'

I take a quick look around. Katie Pierce has vanished. The Year Sevens have all yelled 'Tony!' for nothing.

'*What?*' bellows Walton.

'Our free dinner tickets. We're supposed to be getting them.'

The rest of the Year Sevens start mumbling and grumbling about free dinner tickets.

'*Free dinner tickets?*' shouts Walton.

The Year Sevens shut up.

'Yes please, sir.' Except for this one.

'*Free dinner tickets?*' repeats Walton even louder. '*You get free teachers, free books, free Internet access and now you want free dinner tickets?*'

'Yes, sir, because we were shouting and—'

'*You want free dinner tickets because you were shouting? I've never heard the like in twenty-five years of teaching. Get to my office and wait for me there.*'

'But the girl—'

'*Get to my office. Now!*'

Walton's really giving this kid a good

going over. You've got to admire the kid because he's only little and he keeps eye contact with Walton but you can tell that his chin is beginning to go. Once your chin starts wobbling the tears aren't going to be too far behind. However much you try and blink them back they're going to get out. You just can't trust your body. If it gets a chance it'll let you down.

The kid decides to get along to Walton's office before the waterfall starts. He drops his head and walks off. Walton starts moving down the line, rubbing the queue's nose in how tough he is.

'There are standards in this school. Standards that I expect to be kept. And anyone who decides not to keep to them can go and find a new school today if they want to. Do I make myself clear?'

Same old garbage. Nobody else falls for it apart from Year Sevens. Which reminds me.

'Sharp!'

Too late. I've been so busy watching everything else going on that I've forgotten that I'm openly standing in a queue which is only for Year Sevens. And I've been spotted.

'Sharp, I know that you are a very immature boy but you can't rejoin Year Seven just because

you refuse to grow up and face your responsibilities.'

Walton's still pretty hot and after yesterday I'm hardly his favourite person.

'No doubt you're here to extort money from these children. Those are your targets, aren't they, Sharp? Girls or small boys.'

He seems to have conveniently forgotten that Nicola Cohen told him that I didn't do anything wrong yesterday.

'But I'll wager, Sharp, that if someone your own size stood up to you you'd run a mile. Wouldn't you, Sharp?'

I don't say anything. He's in that mood when he twists everything you say anyway. I just give him a stare.

'Well, I'm not having it, Sharp. These children are in my care and I intend to protect them from you. Now get to my office and wait for me there.'

I shrug my shoulders and get moving. Today really isn't going very well at all.

CHAPTER 20

'Can you stop doing that?'

'Shut up.'

'Nothing's going to happen so just stop it.'

'Shut up.'

'I'll shut up if you stop.'

'Shut up.'

The kid is still crying. He just about held it together in front of Walton but as soon as he got outside his office the tears must have started falling, they were still falling when I got there and they're still falling now, five minutes later. The thing is, it's embarrassing standing outside Walton's office next to a Year Seven who's crying his eyes out. Everybody who goes past thinks the same thing – that we've had a fight and I've made him cry. And I don't want people thinking I'm the kind of guy who goes round beating up Year Sevens. I know it shouldn't matter because I know what the truth is but somehow it still does.

And on top of that his sniffing is really getting on my nerves.

'What's your name?'

'James Young.'

'What are you crying for?'

'Shut up.'

Just when I thought I was getting somewhere.

'Look, nothing bad is going to happen. You just annoyed Walton at the wrong time, that's all. He'll leave you here for a bit and then he'll tell you to go.'

'How do you know?'

'Because I do, all right?'

'But it's so unfair. That girl said about the dinner tickets and I was just asking.'

I feel sorry for the kid. It's tough when you find out for the first time that the world is an unfair place. But we've all got to find out sooner or later because it's not like the world is suddenly going to swap round and start being fair for a change.

'Why is he leaving me out here if he's not going to do anything to me?'

This kid really doesn't know much. So I explain to him how it works. Most teachers reckon that they can get you to crack by making you wait. If they leave you outside a door for half an hour then they figure you'll start imagining all these terrible things that are going to happen to you and by the time they show up you'll be so nervous that you'll admit to anything and do whatever they say just to get the whole thing sorted. It works too until you realize what's going on.

'You're just making that up,' the kid tells me.

You can't help some people. Here I am, kindly giving him the benefit of my understanding of the way that Walton's brain works, and all he does is be rude to me. I'm tempted to tell him that he'll probably get suspended and throw a real scare into him but I don't because an idea flashes across my mind.

'How would you like to get revenge on the girl who got you into trouble?'

'I thought I wasn't in trouble,' snaps back the kid.

He's sharp. You've got to give him that.

'All right, the girl who nearly got you into trouble.'

'Why?'

'Because I can arrange it and revenge makes you feel better.'

'Does it?'

'Of course it does,' I tell him. 'Now listen. I'll do you a deal. If you don't get into any more trouble than a bit of a telling off from Walton then you agree to meet me after school by the filing cabinets at the end of the Humanities corridor and get back at that girl.'

He looks at me. I stare back, trying to give him the impression that I'm the sort of person he should look up to and listen to. I'm not that confident because it's not a look I'm too used to giving. But it's got to be good because my argument stinks. Think about it. I offer him a deal on what Walton does which I can't change anyway. I'm not really offering him anything. But he's a Year Seven. They still do things for credits.

'All right,' he says. 'But you'd better be right about Walton.'

He says that last bit really tough to show that I shouldn't think he's a fool. Which is a shame because by agreeing to the deal he's proving that he is.

'Good,' I say. 'Now what you need to know is . . .'

But I don't get to tell him what he needs to know because I hear Walton coming down the corridor shouting about litter for a change.

I'm right of course. I can read Walton like a book. A big thick book in his case. The kid gets nothing more than a 'Don't interrupt me when I'm talking in future. Now get out of my sight.' It doesn't go quite as well for me. Walton's obviously got it into his brain that I'm into some kind of bullying scam. First I get caught with a clever girl in the toilets and then I get caught in the Year Seven lunch queue. You can tell he knows I'm up to something but he can't figure out what.

He gets me into his office and asks me a few questions but I don't give him anything. Then he tries the long silence with the glare for a bit, hoping that my nerve will go and I'll start blabbing, but I've seen it all before so I just look away. So he tells me to look at him. So I do. Then he tells me to take the insolent look off my face. So I try smiling. Then he tells me this is a very serious matter and to stop. So I do. To be honest I'm a bit insulted. It's not like me and Walton don't know each other and he's still expecting me to fall for this amateur stuff which I rumbled in Year Eight. I deserve a bit more respect.

Anyway, after five minutes he sighs, tells me he's feeling old and weary and gives me a detention right after school. I don't even bother demanding twenty-four hours' notice because I know that last time my dad was up at the school he gave him permission to give me detentions at any time without any notice whatsoever, even over weekends, which I thought was a bit unnecessary.

CHAPTER 21

There's a notice on the staff-room door that says KNOCK AND WAIT, so I knock and start waiting. I'm here because of the idea I had outside Walton's office. I've got the help of the kid and now I need the help of Miss Hardy, my French teacher. I don't plan for her to know she's helping me either.

Another boy comes up. I don't know him. He knocks on the door too and starts waiting. I nod to him. He nods back.

We wait some more.

The thing with knocking on the staff-room door and waiting is that the teachers know it's a kid. Any adult just goes straight in. And teachers never seem big on seeing kids at lunch time. They leave you waiting outside for hours, which isn't exactly polite. But you try ignoring them when they ask you a question in class and they'll go mental at you for being rude.

Finally the door opens and some teacher sticks his bald head out.

'Sir,' I say quickly. 'Is Miss Hardy in there?'

He pops his head back in and then out again. 'She is indeed, young man.'

He doesn't do anything. He just stares at me. I realize that even though he's bald he's got a beard. Why is hair growing at the bottom of his head but not the top? Does it slip down your body as you get older? Do people who are a hundred have it growing out of their feet? That's the sort of stuff they should tell you about in science instead of making you learn all about the reproductive organs of frogs.

'Can you get her for me, sir?'

'You only had to ask,' he says.

The kid next to me opens his bag and gets out a book.

When the door opens again it's Miss Hardy.

'Miss,' I say quickly, 'could I borrow one of the French department tape recorders this afternoon? Would that be OK?'

She looks surprised. 'Why?'

I've got this one all worked out. She's one of these enthusiastic teachers who care about what they're teaching you. She gets terribly upset because nobody understands the past tense and she's been going on about it for about two months now. It's sad really. They shouldn't let people who really like French teach it. It's bound to upset them. I'm sure she'll go for it when she sees one of her kids wanting to do extra work.

'I want to practise my French pronunciation,' I tell her. 'Only it's difficult to tell how you sound if you can't hear yourself so I need a tape recorder. It's time I got down to some hard work in French or else I might fall behind.'

That really is a hot one. I'm already so far behind in French I've been lapped.

She stares hard at me. I try to look as if I'm an enthusiastic pupil but it's one of my looks which has gone a bit rusty.

'And, Mickey, what words exactly were you planning to practise pronouncing?'

'Er . . .' She's got me in a bit of trouble there. I don't know too many words in French.

'I think, Mickey,' she says, 'that we are running before we can walk here. You go away and learn some words and then I'll think about giving you a tape recorder to practise them.'

'But, miss . . .'

'That's my final word, Mickey. *Au revoir.*'

'What?'

'I think I've proved my point. It means goodbye.'

Teachers are so ungrateful. You ask to do more work and they still won't help you.

'Miss Hardy.'

It's the other kid. He's been standing there patiently watching me make a fool of myself.

'Yes, Graham.'

She gives him this big smile. I bet she'd lend him a tape recorder. I bet she'd lend him a whole sound system.

'Will you sign my book? I've got almost all the teachers except you. I'm moving to Milton Keynes next week and this is my last day.'

I was about to go away but when I hear this my legs go all wobbly I'm so shocked. Kids asking teachers for their autographs? What next? Signed posters of the caretaker? Souvenir plasters from the school nurse?

The world is a strange place.

My gran always says, 'Honesty is the best policy.' What she doesn't say is what your back-up policy should be if honesty lets you down. I've been honest. Well, maybe not completely honest but as honest as anybody could expect because I've asked nicely for the tape recorder and Miss Hardy's said no. There's only one option left – dishonesty. I don't want to do it but it's a position I've been forced into. I need a tape recorder and I need it fast. I'm going to have to steal one.

There are loads of tape recorders in our school so it should be really easy to get my hands on one. But I haven't got much time. The bell's going to go for the end of lunch soon. I get down to the languages department fast. All I need to do is find a language teacher and tell her that Miss Hardy has sent me to borrow a tape recorder for the next lesson and I'll have one in a shot. Teachers are always sending kids to get things for them because they're too lazy to carry them about themselves.

But I draw a blank. Every single door is locked. That's typical of the teachers in our school. They never get to lessons on time after lunch. Loads of them are too busy drinking in the pub opposite the school. Mr Kelly was so drunk last year that he fell asleep during Technology. We were doing resistant materials and the morons at the back took the chance to find out how resistant Jack Holland's fingers were when you put them in a vice and tightened it. Not that resistant, it turned out. Mr Kelly took early retirement the next day even though he was only twenty-seven. The school had to give Jack Holland's parents a refund on his piano lessons.

Which reminds me. Which other department always has tape recorders? The music department. I check my watch. There's two minutes left of lunch time. I sprint down the corridor, dodge my way across the concourse and get to the door of Mrs Lennon, who's the Head of Music. We don't have her. We've got Miss McCartney, who's always bursting into tears and telling us that we'll be sorry when she has a nervous breakdown. All the stuff is kept in Mrs Lennon's room because if it was kept in Miss McCartney's it would all be nicked in the first week.

I push the door open slowly. I can't see anybody. But what I can see is music to my eyes. Sitting on Mrs Lennon's desk next to the bust of some dead composer whose nose seems to have fallen off is a sleek, shiny black tape recorder.

By the time I get over to it I realize that it's not so much sleek and shiny as dull and drab but then every bit of school equipment is like that. It doesn't matter how old it is though. I need it. I pick it up and turn round.

And stop.

Behind me is Mrs Lennon. She looks at the tape recorder.

'Miss McCartney sent me to borrow it,' I explain to her.

'No, she didn't,' she tells me.

'She did, miss.'

Mrs Lennon sighs. 'Young man, if Miss McCartney sent you to get this then I am a walrus.'

'What?'

'Miss McCartney is not here today. She is attending a course in South London on the uses of Gangsta Rap in the Modern Music Curriculum.'

I'm in trouble.

'She told me to get it yesterday?' I try.

'Yesterday?'

She doesn't smile back. My troubles look like they're here to stay.

'Attempting to steal school property is very serious—'

'I was only borrowing—'

'Be quiet.'

'But—'

'Quiet.'

I decide that it's a good idea to be quiet.

'What's your name?'

'Philip Mason.' This is no time for the truth.

'Give me your bag, Philip.'

'What?'

The bell goes for the end of lunch.

'I've got to get to my next—'

'Your bag.'

I hand it over. Would you believe it? Mrs Lennon and The Psychos use the same tactics. She pulls out a book and looks at it.

'Philip, you appear to be carrying round the books of Michael Sharp from Nine B in your bag.'

'We've got the same bags, miss. I'm always picking up his and he's always picking up—'

'Quiet.'

'It's quite funny when you . . .'

I stop in the middle of what I'm saying. I'm busted. At least I can try and keep a bit of dignity.

'So, Michael. We'd better be going down to Mr Walton's office. I know he views theft of school property particularly seriously.'

This is appalling. I've already been in front of Walton twice this week. I won't walk out of his office this time. I'll be excluded, maybe even expelled. And there's no escape. She knows my name. She knows my form. She knows everything.

But she's not moving towards the door. Instead she's giving me this strange look.

'Unless . . .'

There's an unless?

'Yes, miss?'

'Mr Walton is very keen that the school has an orchestra, Michael. Prospective parents are very impressed with a school orchestra. I have had great difficulty in recruiting but I have eventually managed to fill all roles but one. I remain in urgent need of a triangle player.'

'The triangle's always been my favourite shape, miss.' Actually I prefer squares.

'Be quiet. If you consent to be this triangle player then perhaps I can delay informing Mr Walton of your actions.'

'Delay, miss?' I was hoping more for stopping altogether.

'Yes, Michael. The delay will last until you miss a rehearsal or a performance or attempt to leave the orchestra by any means what-soever, including deliberately injuring your own hands. The day that happens is the day we go to see Mr Walton. Do I make myself clear?'

I nod.

'Do you agree to join?'

I nod again.

'Welcome to the orchestra, Michael.' She walks past me to her desk and picks up a tape. 'Listen to this at home. It's a very simple piece. Listen to it repeatedly, making a careful note of whenever the triangle is played. Next week is our first rehearsal.'

I can't quite take in what's happened.

'Go on, Michael. Get to your next lesson.'

I'm about to go and then I don't. I've got an idea.

'Miss,' I say, 'the only problem is that my tape recorder at home is bust and I won't be able to listen to the tape unless I can . . . er . . . borrow one.'

I smile at her. She sighs.

'If anything happens to this tape recorder, Michael, then . . .'

'We'll be going to see Mr Walton, miss.'

I grab the recorder, stuff it in my bag and get out of there before she decides to make me a tuba player. Those things look heavy.

CHAPTER 22

Of course I'm late for my next lesson. And Mr Barlow won't believe that I was seeing Mrs Lennon about being the triangle player in the school orchestra. He says it's one of the lamest excuses he's ever heard. So I get another detention. The way they're piling up I figure I might have to stay on an extra year in school just to get them all done. And I haven't had any lunch so I'm starving.

I spend the afternoon thinking about my plan. I know Lejeune and Katie and the rest of his team are doing dodgy things to try and win this election but I've got to have proof. Proof that I can give to Carl Marks to give to Walton so that he will have to disqualify Lejeune. I heard Katie tell Lejeune about a strategy meeting in room 19 after school. There's a good chance that they'll talk about what they've been up to. If I can get a recorder hidden in the room then I'll have the proof I need. I want James Young to put the tape recorder in there because if anybody sees me and tells Katie Pierce or Nicola Cohen they'll start hearing alarm bells. But nobody ever thinks Year Sevens are up to anything. They're just too little.

So I sit through the afternoon wondering whether little James Young will let me down. He seemed brave enough but he might also be clever enough to work out that there is nothing in the deal for him but revenge. Between lessons I check out room 19. There's a cupboard which looks perfect for the job. I can get James to stick the tape recorder in there. We have Geography last. I grab the seat right by the door even though it's at the front so that I can get out fast. We get to compare the average rainfall in Birmingham, Manchester and Glasgow so the time just zooms by. I only feel about two years older by the time the bell goes for the end of school.

I am out of that door fast and running down towards the Humanities corridor. It's never that easy getting anywhere quickly straight after school's finished because everybody's charging for the exits. If you saw the speed kids move to get away from the classrooms you'd think there had been a bomb scare. Except that when there is a bomb scare everybody takes their time because the longer it takes the more of the lesson you miss. So that's not really the best comparison.

Despite my running James Young beats me to the filing cabinets just down the corridor from room 19. Looks like he's up for it.

'Hello,' he says.

'We've got no time for that,' I tell him firmly because he's Year Seven and I'm Year Nine and he needs to look up to me.

'Oh,' he says.

'Take this tape recorder into room nineteen. Put it in the white cupboard on the left and press record. Wedge the microphone in the crack of the door so it sticks out just a tiny bit and get out of there fast. You've probably got about three minutes. OK?'

I'm ready to repeat it because he's in Year Seven so he probably won't understand it the first time but I don't need to. He nods, grabs the tape recorder and goes.

It happens so fast that I stand there for a second not knowing what to do. And then I realize that there isn't anything. For once I've got to trust someone else to do it for me. All I can do is get out of sight and wait.

I push a filing cabinet forward slightly and

slip behind it. Then I shift the other one forward a tiny bit. In the tiny gap between them I can see the door to room 19.

James Young has gone in but he hasn't come out. This is good news. It means that the room's empty. All he has to do is get the stuff set up – it can't take him long. And then at the other end of the corridor walking down to room 19 I see Lejeune. James Young's got about fifteen seconds to get out of the room. It doesn't matter if Lejeune sees him leaving – he won't suspect anything. All that matters is that James Young sets it up and gets clear. Lejeune gets closer to room 19. This is my last chance to get any evidence. The school election is tomorrow morning. Come on, James. Get out.

He doesn't. Lejeune walks straight up to the door and pushes it open.

'Tony.'

A miracle. Down the corridor come Katie Pierce and Julie Reece. Lejeune turns round and lets the door close. This is the kid's chance. I wait for the door to open.

It doesn't.

I can't believe it. How stupid can this kid be? Katie and Julie walk up to Lejeune. They go into the classroom together. I can't take my eyes off the door but still nobody is coming out. What is going on?

Over the next couple of minutes a few more kids I recognize from Lejeune's campaign team go into room 19. Surely they'd have thrown James Young out by now. But even though nobody comes out someone very important goes in. The someone who goes in confirms an awful lot. Because that someone is Nicola Cohen. She doesn't stay in there more than a minute but I figure that's long enough for her to pass on what she needs to and get her orders. Conclusive proof she's been two-facing me. All that garbage about her job and journalistic standards and crying when she's been playing me for a fool and working for Tony Lejeune the whole time. His whole organization is even nastier than I'd figured, which reminds me that I ought to start worrying about the Year Seven kid I've left stuck in the middle of it.

Ten minutes, then fifteen. I ask myself whether there's another door out of room 19. It's a stupid question. I've had PSE in that room for a whole year and I'd have noticed. I look at my watch for the two millionth time. Seventeen minutes forty-eight seconds. I put my eye back to the gap between the filing cabinets as the door opens and out walks Katie Pierce.

The whole corridor is deserted and silent. I stop breathing. It's strange. As soon as she's outside the classroom she stops. And then slowly she turns round in a circle looking all around her. The door opens again. Julie Reece comes out. Then they both turn round in a circle. What has happened in that class-room? Is there some kind of demonic force in room 19 which has possessed all the people who've gone in there?

'Mickey.'

For one tiny bit of a part of a second I thought it was the devil calling me. Then I realized it was Katie Pierce. Finding out it was her didn't make it much better.

'Mickey!' She shouts out my name in this horrible, syrupy, mocking voice and it echoes down the empty corridor. 'We know you're there, Mickey.'

I decide to keep down. You never know. She might be bluffing.

'Are you looking for this, Mickey?'

And she holds up a tape. And as the tape goes up the last of my hopes chokes, wheezes horribly and dies.

'We've got your little friend, Mickey. Don't you want to come and see him?'

And Katie and Julie laugh. They've got me. There's no way I can leave a little Year Seven kid in their hands. I've known Katie a long time and I've got a pretty good idea of the torments she could inflict on little James Young. I've seen her reduce Year Eleven lads with tattoos of guns on their necks to tears. If I don't stand up he'll probably be terrified of girls for the rest of his life. I push the filing cabinet to one side and come out.

They're at one end of the corridor. I'm at the other. We face each other like gunfighters in those old films they put on the telly on Saturday afternoon.

'Look what's crawled out of that grubby corner, Julie.'

'Is it a worm, Katie?'

'Or a cockroach, Julie?'

'Or a hamster, Katie?'

Katie stops looking contemptuously at me for a second and glares at Julie. 'A hamster?'

'I don't like hamsters.'

'Leave the talking to me,' says Katie. 'Concentrate on staring. You can probably just about manage that.' She turns back to me. 'No, it's a dark, ugly, troll-like creature.

194

There's only one boy in this school who's so ugly that he has to hide his face behind furniture. Hello, Mickey.'

'Hello, Katie.' I smile to show her that I don't care.

'Getting little kids to do your work for you these days, are you? Not enough of a man to do it yourself?'

'He wasn't supposed to—'

'I know we've had our differences before, Mickey, but I've always respected you. At least then you weren't skulking in the shadows while Year Seven kids did all the work. You were always stupid, Mickey, but I didn't think you were a coward as well.'

'I'm not a coward,' I tell them. 'Now you've had your fun. Hand over the kid. He didn't know what he was doing. Your argument is with me. Let the kid go.'

'The troll is giving us orders, Julie.'

'I'm scared, Katie.'

'I'm terrified, Julie. We'd better do what he says or he might do something really frightening like hiding behind a filing cabinet.'

Katie nods to Julie who knocks on the door of room 19. The door opens a tiny bit and little James Young gets pushed out. He's trying to hide it but you can see that he's been crying. He's got this serious face on.

'I'm sorry.'

'Don't worry about it,' I tell him.

'I meant to get out in time but when the door opened I squashed myself in the cupboard but then they came in and I got the tape recorder going and it was going fine but the only thing was that I was late for lunch because Mr Walton was telling me off and they only had one thing left and it was beans and so I had a double portion and you know what beans do to you and I kept saying to myself, Hold on, hold on, and then just when I wasn't thinking it came out and it made a big noise and they opened the cupboard and found me.'

He says all this at a hundred miles an hour and when he's finished he's crying again. I feel bad. I didn't mean him to get into a cupboard and get all upset.

'We did you a favour getting you out,' Katie tells him. 'That thing really stank.'

'And then they kept asking me why I was there and then she said that if I didn't tell them they'd report me to Mr Walton for being in a cupboard and they'd send me to a special school for mad kids who hide in cupboards and wardrobes and I'd never get any qualifications, just souvenir coat hangers. And I would have done it and gone to a school for people who hide in cupboards and wardrobes because I'd do that rather than tell her anything but I couldn't face my mum and my dad and my sister finding out. They'd be so upset and so I told her.'

If I felt bad before I feel terrible now. 'Go home, kid,' I say.

He looks up at me and his eyes are angry. 'Stop calling me kid,' he shouts. 'My name is James Young.'

And he holds his head up, turns his back on me and walks off down the corridor. We all watch him in silence until he disappears down the stairs.

'That was touching,' says Katie. 'I feel like I might cry.'

'Shut up,' I tell her.

'Now, now, Mickey. Don't get angry.'

I know I shouldn't get mad. It's the easiest way to let a cold-hearted girl like Katie Pierce get the better of you. But sometimes you don't have a choice.

'I'll get you for this, Katie. I know what you're doing with this election. Tony Lejeune will never be Head Boy.'

'Won't he, Mickey?' she says and she moves closer to me. 'With the votes being cast first thing tomorrow morning and no proof of any cheating? Would you like to make a bet?'

Her eyes look into mine. I will myself not to look away.

'Well?'

I look away.

'Thought so,' she says. 'All mouth, no trousers. Go back to your hole, little troll.'

I hear her and Julie walking away. As they go down the stairs their laughter floats up to remind me that I'm beaten.

CHAPTER 23

What you don't need when you've totally blown a case is to head home for a Coke and a packet of crisps and find the guy who gave you the case in the first place standing outside your shed.

'I hadn't heard from you,' Carl says. 'And time's running out.'

I lead him inside and motion him to the box. He stays standing.

'I haven't got much time,' he tells me. 'There are many things to do before tomorrow morning. Tell me how things are going.'

If I was honest I'd have to say disastrous, hopeless, terrible, awful and any other long words I can think of meaning bad. But nobody gets anywhere telling the truth at a time like this.

'The investigation is proceeding,' I tell him. I heard some policeman say that on the news.

'What does that mean?' Unfortunately the reporter didn't ask that question.

'It means that it's ongoing,' I say.

'I know it's ongoing,' Carl Marks points out. 'I'm paying for it to be ongoing. What have you learnt?'

'I have a number of new leads,' I tell him, 'and I will be following them up. I'll let you know as soon as something develops.'

'The election is tomorrow.'

'That's a good point.'

'So I need to know what you've found out. And I need to know now.'

He's paying the bills. I'm going to have to tell him.

So I do. I tell him all about what's happened to me during the day and what I think is going on and who I think is behind it.

'What?' He bangs his fist on the table. 'You bugged my opponent's private strategy meeting and then you got caught? Do you know who you've made me look like?'

I shake my head.

'Only the most disgraced politician in the history of the free world. They will investigate the bugging. The trail will lead back to me. I'll be disgraced. I'll never be able to run for political office again.'

'What are you talking about?' I tell him.

'They're cheating. All I was trying to do was catch them.'

'My political career is over. I shall withdraw from the election at the hustings tomorrow morning. I will give a full and frank account of all that has happened. There will be no whitewash in this shed.'

I agree with him there. My dad never gets round to painting anything.

'It's my fault. The buck stops with me. I should never have trusted you.' He shakes his head so violently it looks like it's going to come off. 'I should have fought this campaign honestly instead of descending to the gutter tactics of my opponent, employing a shady sleuth to spy on my behalf. I shall devote the rest of my life to charitable works.'

I think he's going mad.

'It's not that big a deal,' I say. 'You didn't know about it and it didn't even work.'

'Shut up,' he says. 'I have nothing further to say to you. I will speak to the electors of Hanford High at assembly tomorrow and tell them of your disgusting schemes and of my foolish indulgence of them. We may both be disgraced but at least I will be disgraced with dignity.'

And he walks out, slamming the door behind him.

I'm off the case again. I lean back in my chair and pull out a packet of crisps and a bottle of Coke. You win some, you lose some. After the day I've had I'm almost happy to forget about it. But I'm not even halfway through my first packet of cheese 'n' onion when the door opens again and standing there is Nicola Cohen.

'Hi, Mickey,' she says, shutting the door behind her.

She's got some nerve, I'll give her that. She's destroyed my case, made me look a fool, hired The Psychos to sit on my head and yet she's still in the mood to come round and say hello.

'How did you find me?' I ask. 'Some of your friends tell you where I might be?'

'I'm an investigative journalist, Mickey. We find things out.'

'Yeah,' I say. 'Well, detectives find things out too.'

'What's with your attitude?' she asks.

I've got to give it to her. She plays the innocent really well. But she's not going to play me any more.

'I would have thought you could work

that out since you're such a good journalist.'

She thinks for a second. Or at least she pretends to think for a second. 'You're not still angry about what I said at lunch time, are you?' she asks. 'You've got to admit, Mickey, that thinking Mr Walton was behind it all was pretty dumb. But I've spent the afternoon looking into the whole case and I think that a lot of what you said really adds up.'

'You don't say,' I tell her.

'I do. And I've found out some other stuff too. I think it all links together with some of what you were saying and, if we work together on this, we might just get the whole story before it's too late. I've got one bit to chase up and there's another bit for you and—'

'And,' I interrupt her, 'it will be a big surprise if my bit leads all the way to The Psychos and I get another beating. Is that what we're saying, Nicola?'

'What?' She looks puzzled.

'Very good,' I tell her. 'I'd could almost believe you if I hadn't seen you going into Tony Lejeune's strategy meeting after school today.'

'What?'

'I saw you. Room nineteen. Straight after school.'

'We had Maths in there last lesson. I forgot my calculator. I just went back to get it.'

'Yeah?'

'I'll show you my timetable,' she says and she pulls her bag off her shoulder, dumps it on my desk and starts rummaging in it. All of me knows she's lying. She starts chucking things on my desk, then going back into her bag to look some more. Her lunch box, her books and her pencil case. Everything's really neat. There's no graffiti on any of the books and her handwriting is perfect. But however tidy it all is it doesn't make her tactics any better. I've seen this approach before. In fact I've tried it before. It's what I do when I'm trying to con a teacher that I've really done my homework but just forgotten it. Sometimes if you make it look really good and empty your whole bag they believe you.

'I can't find it,' she says. 'I must have left it at home.'

'What a coincidence,' I tell her. 'So now you've got nothing to back up your story.'

'Hey.' She stops putting the stuff back in her bag and looks at me. 'I don't need anything to back up my story. I'm telling the truth and if you can't see that then you're even more of a fool than I thought you were earlier today when you were telling me that Mr Walton was at the top of a conspiracy to rig the Head Boy contest.'

She's hit me at my weakest point there. Now that I know that he wasn't behind it the whole idea does sound a bit dumb.

'Just because I was wrong once doesn't mean that I'm going to be wrong for ever,' I tell her. 'I know who's behind it all now.'

'So do I,' she tells me. 'I found out what's been going on at the school paper.'

I can't believe she's still got the nerve to try and lie it out. I can feel myself getting angry.

'Yeah, but it wasn't too hard for you to find out, was it?' I point out. 'Seeing as how you were involved. You set me up to get a beating. You were working for Tony Lejeune the whole time.'

'What?' she gasps.

'Don't try the shocked look on me,' I tell her. 'You're not a proper journalist. You just write lies.'

She's starting to look really mad. The shot about writing lies looks like it's really got to her.

'Oh yeah, you know, you know all right!'

she yells. 'You know nothing, do you understand? Nothing at all.'

She grabs the last of her stuff off the desk and crushes it into her bag. She wrenches open the door of the shed and then turns back. 'You know what's stupid?'

I shrug as though I couldn't care.

'I didn't think you were like the other morons in our school. I thought you were OK.'

She slams the door as she goes out. You've got to give the girl points for her drama skills. Even though I knew all about her involvement she didn't give anything away. And her big pay-off line before she slammed the door? I bet she heard that in a lousy movie or read it in some pathetic book. It almost makes me laugh. But it doesn't because I liked her. I liked her way more than I should have done and it messed up my judgement. If I'd seen through her earlier on I might have solved the whole thing. It's not like it's my first case. I should know by now that rule number one is not to get emotionally involved. You get emotionally involved and you end up wanting someone like Walton to be guilty and wanting someone like Nicola to be innocent. You've got to stay independent. But I let myself be taken in by her. Just because she was tough and clever and good-looking.

I can't stay in the shed. I screw up my empty crisp packet and chuck it towards the bin. I miss, which shouldn't surprise me. I don't bother to pick it up. The way I feel right now I don't see that there's much chance I'll be using this shed for anything in future. Especially not for being a detective.

I head into the house for my tea but just as I open the back door something triggers a thought in my mind. I don't know what does it but I know there's something I've just seen which is important. Something to do with Nicola Cohen. Something to do with what she's just shown me. Something she got out of her bag. Her books. No, not exactly her books. Something on her books. Her hand-writing. I've seen it somewhere before.

But I can't click on exactly where and I'm not really in the mood to try too hard to remember. I'm off the case and whatever it is isn't going to change anything. I'm sick of the whole thing. I'm determined to get into a massive argument with my dad. With any luck he'll call me loads of names and send me to my room. I'm so annoyed with myself at the moment that it's exactly what I need.

I go in through the kitchen and into the dining room.

'Where have you been?' demands my mum.

'You're late,' my dad tells me.

This is starting out just the way I need it to. I shrug to keep it going.

'Don't shrug at your mother,' snaps my dad. 'Eat your tea.'

'Eat it quickly, Mickey,' adds my mum. 'We've got to be there in half an hour.'

'Where?'

'Your parents' evening.'

I choke on my first mouthful of pizza. How could I have forgotten? Parents' evening. The worst evening of every year. And I've managed to arrange it so that it's neatly following the worst day. Great timing, Mickey, great timing.

CHAPTER 24

'Would you say that was fair, Mickey?'

'What?' I'd switched off for a minute.

'What I just said.'

'Which bit?'

'Well, all of it really.'

I look at Mr Newman hoping he'll give me some help. I'd been trying to listen, I really had. But I've already sat through Miss Hardy, Miss Hurley and Mr Lynch telling my parents that I'm lazy, unfocused, determined to waste my potential, lacking intellectual curiosity, behind with my class work, behind with my homework, depressing to have in their room and the sort of child who makes them wish they could take early retirement, and after a while all the things they say start to wash over you and sound the same.

'Answer Mr Newman,' says my mum.

'Sit up straight,' says my dad.

I've got no option. I sit up straight and tell Mr Newman that I think whatever he said was fair.

'Good,' he says. 'So now we all agree that you have some intelligence and you are capable of making progress what we've got to sort out is what is stopping you. There must be a problem that's more deep seated than school. Wouldn't you agree, Mickey?'

'Yes,' I tell him even though I don't.

I hate the way teachers do this at parents' evenings. They pretend they're asking you questions which you can answer any way you like when they know that if you don't say exactly what they want you to say then, as soon as you're out of the school hall, your parents will kill you.

'So how can we crack this problem?' asks Newman. 'How can we move Mickey from being an unwilling conscript in the education system to being a willing volunteer?'

'Bring back the cane,' suggests my dad eagerly.

'I don't think—' begins Mr Newman.

'Not for everyone. Just him. I wouldn't sue anyone. I'll even buy the cane.'

'Mr Sharp, I'm afraid this isn't . . .'

'When I was at school if you didn't do your classwork they hit you. If you didn't do your homework they hit you.'

'I see, Mr Sharp,' says Newman, 'but I don't see where this is getting us.'

'Look at this country,' says my dad. 'It used to be a place you could be proud of, a place you could respect and now it's a dump filled with drug addicts and criminals and overpaid footballers.'

'Coming back to Mickey,' says Mr Newman. 'What do we think it is that's stopping him committing himself fully in school?'

There's a pause while we all try and think of an answer. Well actually, while they try and think of the answer. I know what the answer is but telling them would get me nowhere. The reason I don't want to do any work at school is because it's so pointless. Soil erosion in the Nile Delta. Rainfall in Glasgow. Where you should put a comma. Why people built canals. Why people stopped building canals. Venn diagrams. Angles. The periodic table. Photosynthesis.

It is all so boring.

What would happen if they made adults sit down for six hours a day and listen to grumpy teachers drone on and on about loads of stuff that nobody wants to know about? They'd all refuse to go. But when you're a kid they say it's the law. The only reason they made going to school the law was because otherwise nobody would have turned up. History teachers try telling you that otherwise we'd all have to sweep chimneys and be exploited but it's not true. Everybody's got central heating now so they don't need anybody to sweep chimneys. They make it the law to go to school because otherwise we'd all do something more interesting instead.

But try explaining that to your parents or a teacher. They can't cope when you tell them the truth.

'Come on, Mickey,' says Mr Newman. 'You know more about this than the rest of us. What's going on in your head?'

I go for the obvious answer. I'm not proud of it but the only way to get people like teachers and parents to stop nagging you is to tell them what they want to hear.

'I think I'm going through a sort of phase, sir,' I say.

He nods. My mum nods. My dad looks like he wants to hit me.

'Adolescence,' says Mr Newman.

'Hormones,' says my mum.

'Personal hygiene problems,' adds my dad.

I don't react. I've got another five teachers after this one and if I'm going to survive I've got to try and sell everybody on the idea that I'm a troubled adolescent who needs sympathy more than punishment, so that I don't end up on drugs and in trouble with the police. I've got to make them see my whole situation could be lots worse so let's live with what we've got.

'So, Mickey,' says Mr Newman. 'How do we get past this phase?'

'Do you think school is the answer?' butts in my dad.

I'm surprised. It isn't every day that your dad says something that makes sense.

'How do you mean, Mr Sharp?' asks Newman.

'I was just thinking,' says my dad.

'Yes?' says Mr Newman.

'My eldest brother, Mickey's Uncle Pop. He lives on a farm on the west coast of Ireland. Very remote it is. Nothing for miles except the sea and the land and the mountains and the sheep. We could send him there for a year.'

I don't like the sound of this one bit.

'Mmmm,' muses Mr Newman. 'I'm not sure that's legal. You mean a sort of year out?'

'Well, out of my hair,' says my dad.

This is getting way out of hand.

'Hey,' I say. 'I don't want to go to the west coast of nowhere.'

'I think our ten minutes is up,' says Mr Newman quickly.

'It would do you good,' says my dad.

'I don't like the country.'

'What you like and what you don't like aren't going to matter for much longer, Mickey.'

'My next appointment's waiting,' interjects Mr Newman, who's rapidly lost interest in my adolescent problems.

'Come on,' says my mum.

'I'm not going anywhere until he says I don't have to go to Uncle Pop's farm.'

My mum gives my dad a look. He tries to pretend he doesn't see it but then he shakes his head to show that he doesn't agree with what he's about to say.

'All right,' he says. 'But if I have any more people from this school complaining about you then you'll be spending the next year talking to sheep. You understand?'

I nod.

'Well, I'm glad we've reached a conclusion which satisfies everyone,' says Mr Newman.

'See you next year.'

Finally my parents get up to go.

'Oh at last,' says the woman next in the queue. 'I hope you realize that you've over-run by three and a half minutes.'

'We're very sorry,' my mum tells her.

'Sorry is hardly adequate,' the woman snaps back. 'My son has dyslexia you know.'

My mum turns to my dad. 'Who's next?'

'His Maths teacher,' says my dad.

A horrible thought suddenly occurs to me.

'Will his opinion be better, Mickey?'

A really terrible thought. It's so awful that the whole world seems to be spinning around me.

'Are you listening, Mickey?

'Sorry, Mum, I've got to go to the toilet. I'll catch up with you later.'

And I go before they can stop me. I've just put two and two together and made disaster. Tomorrow at assembly Carl Marks is going to stand up in front of the whole school and withdraw from the election. And he's going to explain why. And he's going to talk about my part in the whole thing. And Walton's going to hear. And Walton's going to walk straight out of that assembly and pick up the phone and ring my dad. And I'm going to be on the boat to the west coast of nowhere.

I can't let that happen. If I can just get some proof that they've been cheating then maybe I can get Lejeune disqualified before Carl Marks can withdraw. Maybe that will get Carl Marks to shut up. It's my only hope.

Except I don't have a clue how to get any proof. I admitted to myself when Katie Pierce destroyed the tape that I was finished. There's no time left to solve the case and no evidence to get. I've been in bad situations before but this is the worst.

I've been walking while I've been thinking and I've ended up in an empty corridor. A corridor I've walked down loads of times without even thinking about it, but if Carl Marks drops me in it tomorrow I might never get to walk down it again. It's the corridor where we have religious studies and there's a display on the wall with pictures of people from different religions drawn by kids. There's God with a white beard and Jesus with a black one and Shiva dancing and Moses with his two tablets of stone and Buddha sitting with his legs crossed and some others whose names I can't remember. Above all these pictures it says, HANFORD HIGH: PROMOTING RELIGIOUS TOLERANCE AND

HARMONY. Miss Hastings, our RS teacher, wouldn't put my picture up because I drew the devil. She said the devil wasn't part of the modern curriculum. She takes religion very seriously. She says that if people were more religious then the problems of the world would all be solved. But I'm looking at this picture of all these religious people and it doesn't seem to be solving mine.

Above the display something moves. I look up. A CCTV camera. You only notice them when it's quiet and they move to get a shot of the other side of the corridor like the other one did a couple of days ago when Miss Hurley sent me out of class.

And then a bubble bursts inside my head with a great big exclamation mark in it.

First I sprint to the Maths corridor where I put up the poster. There's one there.

Next I head for the corridor outside the dining room. There's one there.

All the time I'm thinking about the tape with TUESDAY written on that the secretary brought into Walton's office while I was getting unfairly told off for trying to kill Nicola Cohen. They must work on a weekly system. One tape for each day, which isn't erased until the next week. That

217

means that the evidence will still be there.

All I need to do is get those tapes. Unfortunately they're in Walton's office and I'm going to have to get them out. But there isn't any other option. And I've got a chance. Parents' evenings are one of the few times when everyone's in the main hall and the rest of the school is empty. I should be able to get in and out of Walton's office without being caught.

'Michael.'

CHAPTER 25

There aren't many people who call me that. I turn round. Behind me is Mrs Lennon.

'Sorry, miss,' I say. 'I've got to go. My mum and dad are waiting for me.'

'They'll have to wait a little longer, Mickey. I need you.'

'But miss . . .'

'Now, Michael, or Mr Walton will be hearing from me.'

'What do you want?'

'Don't speak to me like that, Michael. I want you to take your place in the first performance by the Year Nine orchestra.'

'What?' I'm shocked. 'But the first rehearsal isn't till next week, miss. I haven't even listened to the tape you gave me. I don't even know what a triangle looks like.'

Perhaps that's pushing it too far.

'Now, Michael, I know this must be a bit of a shock to you. If I'm completely honest it's a shock to me. There has been a little confusion between myself and Mr Walton. He is sure that I informed him last year that the Year Nine orchestra would be ready for its first performance on parents' evening, whereas I was under the impression that the first performance would be at the awards ceremony. He is very much of the opinion that the orchestra has to make its debut this evening.'

'But I can't play—'

'All that has been taken care of. You're the last I've had to find. All you have to do is come with me and join the others and hold your triangle.'

'But I've got—'

'Michael.'

She holds all the cards. I follow her.

The orchestra is sitting on the stage at the back of the assembly hall. I thought orchestras were supposed to have loads of musicians in but this one hasn't. There's two boys with violins and some girl with a cello. One girl with a flute is next to a guy with a clarinet and there are three girls with trumpets and trombones. Behind them all is one of the morons at the back. He's got some huge timpani drums.

'Here's your triangle, Michael,' Mrs Lennon says. 'Just pretend to hit it now and then.'

'Pretend?'

'Yes,' she says. 'Didn't I mention you'd be miming?'

'Miming?'

'Yes,' she says. 'Like pop stars do.'

'But, miss, we'll look stupid.'

'Nonsense. It's only a short piece. We'll keep all the parents at a distance and nobody will ever know.'

This is going to be so humiliating. I'm going to have to stand up in front of the whole year and all their parents and mime playing the triangle.

'You stand next to the drum as you're a member of the percussion section.'

I walk up the steps to the stage like a zombie and take my position next to the moron at the back. I keep my triangle behind me.

The moron at the back looks at me. 'What did she get you for?'

Normally I don't talk to the morons at the back but this is an exception. 'Borrowing a tape recorder.'

He nods. 'She got me for gluing a piano lid down.' He indicates the girl with the flute. 'She lit a fire inside a guitar. We're all in here for something.'

I can't believe it. Mrs Lennon has assembled the entire orchestra by threatening to expose them to Mr Walton for bad behaviour if they don't join. There must be a law against doing that.

'Ladies and gentleman.'

I look up. Walton is standing at the front of the stage. Everybody in the hall has turned round to look at him.

'Despite what many of you may have read in our last OFSTED report this school is one which prides itself on making cultural events for the students a central part of its curriculum. I would therefore ask you to pause for a few minutes to witness the first performance of the Year Nine orchestra, giving us a short piece entitled . . . remind me what it's called, Mrs Lennon.'

'Caprice on a Rococo Theme for Strings and Triangle,' she tells him.

'Exactly,' agrees Walton. 'Please don't approach the stage as the music will travel to you. Ladies and gentleman, the Year Nine orchestra.'

Everybody lifts up their instruments. Not knowing what else to do I pull out my triangle. Suddenly from behind us the music starts. The kids who haven't quite managed to get their instruments into position jam them into their mouths. They all start blowing or scraping or at least pretending to. I ping my triangle. I can hear it but with the classical noise coming out from behind me nobody in the audience can. All they can hear is the backing track.

After about thirty seconds I get up the nerve to look round properly. All the parents in the hall are watching us in a strange way that you don't see often from adults. It's almost as though they admire us. I see my mum and dad and even they're looking proud. I'm ashamed to admit it but when I see them looking at me I kind of puff my chest out. It's embarrassing but I do it. My parents haven't looked proud of me since I was six.

And then the moron on the drums hits the girl with the flute on the head with his stick. The girl swings round and catches the boy with the clarinet in the face with her flute. The boy with the clarinet topples backwards into the drums. One of the drums rolls off its stand and careers into the kids with the violins. The kids with the violins leap up and start shouting at the moron on the drums. He shouts back. The girl with the flute screams

223

for help because the boy with the clarinet appears to have got it stuck in his mouth when he fell backwards and is starting to go blue.

All that's left of the orchestra is me and my triangle. I keep pinging away but one triangle does not explain all the classical music pouring out of the speakers behind me.

There's a rush of teachers onto the stage. One teacher pulls the violinists off the drummer. Another tries to comfort the girl with the flute. Another yanks the clarinet out of the boy's throat and starts giving him mouth-to-mouth resuscitation. The boy weakly tries to fight him off. Even death is preferable to being snogged by a teacher.

And then the music stops.

The sudden sound of silence makes the whole place seem extra quiet. Everybody in the room is staring at the stage. I'm the only one looking back. You feel strange when a whole room is looking at you. You feel like you ought to do something. So I do.

I bow.

Nobody applauds.

All they do is keep staring. Maybe they don't appreciate culture.

Walton pushes past me and rushes to the front of the stage. 'Ladies and gentlemen, parents, friends of the school,' he announces. 'There has obviously been some kind of hiccup in the proceedings. Rest assured that none of the children were harmed during the making of this musical event. Please return to the interviews with your children's teachers. Rejoin your queues now, please.'

There's a moment's silence. You can tell that everyone in the hall wants to know what was going on. All it'll take is one question and they'll all join in. But nobody asks it. After a couple of seconds they all start heading back to the teachers' desks muttering to each other.

This is a golden chance. If I move quickly while everything's still confused I could get what I need.

I slip out of the hall and down to Walton's office. Nobody's around. I sneak in. I need to get the videos fast. If I'm caught going through stuff in Walton's office we'd be talking expulsion and the police. No wonder my heart is banging away and I've got this taste as if I'm going to be sick.

I can't see them on his desk. I start opening the drawers. All they've got inside is pens and papers and stuff, apart from the bottom one, which has got a half-drunk bottle of whisky, but no videos. I get over to the cupboard and yank it open. There they are all neatly lined up: MONDAY, TUESDAY, WEDNESDAY, THURSDAY, FRIDAY. I only need TUESDAY and THURSDAY so I grab them and jam them into the pockets of my coat. But I'm nervous and I drop TUESDAY. And as I bend down to pick it up the door opens.

'If you'd care to step into my office we could discuss it.'

It's Walton's voice. What am I going to do? There's no talking my way out of this. I'm finished. And then I remember James Young. Do what he did.

'This way,' says Walton. 'Do sit down.'

The cupboard door won't click shut. I have to hold onto it from the inside, which is impossible because there's nothing to grip except a tiny clip. But when the only other choice is being expelled and arrested sometimes you can manage to do impossible things. I hold onto it with everything I've got and somehow the door doesn't open.

'It's about your son,' Walton says.

'Thought so,' says a voice.

'Oh dear,' says another voice.

They are voices I recognize. They belong to my mum and dad. I almost let go of the tiny clip but I don't. Getting caught now would be even worse.

'Would you consider sending him to a new school?' says Walton.

'What?' says my dad.

'Why?' says my mum.

'Well, Mrs Sharp, Mickey is obviously not happy at Hanford.'

'That's OK,' my dad says. 'He's not happy at home either. He's moody.'

I can't believe this. Aren't your parents supposed to stand up for you?

'Oh,' says Walton, sounding a bit surprised. 'Well, there's also the fact that he's underachieving academically. When he arrived at school in Year Seven our initial tests showed he was quite bright and yet his results have collapsed over the last year. Unfortunately these are the kind of statistics that school inspectors tend to notice and it doesn't reflect well on the school. I'm sure a fresh start would benefit everyone.'

'I don't know,' says my mum.

'We could make it worth your while.'

I don't believe this. Is Walton actually trying to bribe my parents to get me out of the school? They can't put up with that.

'How much?' asks my dad.

They can.

'I'm not talking money here, Mr Sharp.'

'Oh.'

'Mickey's school record is not a pretty sight. There are many incidents of poor behaviour. If you were to agree to move him to another school then perhaps those records could be mislaid and Mickey would leave Hanford as a pupil without a stain on his reputation. Nobody would ever know.'

I always knew adults were devious but this is disgraceful. I'm so angry I want to jump out of the cupboard and shout at all three of them. But getting angry is a mistake. Because when I get angry my hands start to sweat and can't grip the tiny clip any more. It slips out of my fingers. With a slow, screeching creak the cupboard door swings open.

My mum, my dad and Walton all look at me. None of them says anything. I don't think I'll bow this time.

'Hello,' I try. I try a friendly smile.

'What are you doing in that cupboard?' shout three voices at once.

It's a good question.

'Er . . . hiding.'

'Hiding?' shouts Walton. 'Hiding in your Head Teacher's cupboard? Hiding from what?'

That's an even better question.

'Yes, hiding from what?' says my mum.

I look at her.

'From what?' demands my father.

I look at all of them. This is no time for my brain to let me down. There must be a way out. There must be a reason. I just need my brain to tell it to me. Come on, brain.

'Mum ... Dad ...' Come on, brain. 'Mr Walton ...' Come on, brain. 'I'm ...' Come on, brain. 'I'm ... I'm ... I'm being bullied.'

Thank you, brain.

And then I start crying.

CHAPTER 26

I'm dead. I don't know when or where it's going to happen but I know that it is. And I signed my own death warrant. It was me who told them last night that I was hiding in Walton's cupboard because I was afraid of getting beaten up by The Psychos. It was the only thing I could think of that would hold everything together. I told them I'd seen The Psychos were outside the school and panicked and thought they were going to come for me. When they asked me why I'd hidden in Walton's office I had to tell them that I thought the Head Teacher's office was the safest place.

You could tell they didn't believe me. But because I kept crying none of them was prepared to be the first actually to say I was lying. Just in case there was a minuscule 0.0001% chance that I might be telling the truth. After a bit Walton told my parents that he would investigate my allegations next morning and my mum and dad took me home and I cried all the way. It's a skill I never knew I had, crying to order – it sort of happened. I kept it going all the way back and I didn't stop until I got into my bedroom. It got me out of that mess but it got me into another. And that situation is much worse. The Psychos. When they find out that I've grassed them up I am history.

But if I'm going to die I'm going to die having solved this case. I'm too near to cracking it to walk away now. I've finally got the evidence.

It's like this. I'd already got the videos in my coat pockets when they caught me. And Walton was so shocked to see me that he didn't notice they were missing. The next thing I have to do is watch them. This is tough. Having just gone upstairs crying my eyes out I can't exactly pop straight down and say, 'Mind if I use the video?' So I have to wait until everyone is asleep. I set my alarm for 3 a.m. and lie down. The next thing I hear is the tinny squeal of my watch. I wait until I'm certain nobody else has woken up and then I sneak downstairs to check out what I've got.

And what I've got is dynamite.

* * *

The next day on my way to school I keep checking all around me for the blond hair and sunglasses that mean The Psychos. I know that they won't know yet. Walton told my parents that he'd get round to the investigation some time in the morning and would ring them up when he'd established the facts. The big Friday assembly happens right at the start of the day, with the elections for Head Boy and Head Girl straight afterwards. There's no way that Walton would get to The Psychos before then. But knowing that in my brain doesn't stop my body feeling nervous. And the closer I get to school the worse it gets.

I've changed my plan too. When I first saw the evidence I thought I should take it to Walton. But I figure if I take it to him now I'll never get a chance to show it. He'll catch on straight off that I nicked the videos from his office and that I was lying last night about being bullied and he'll probably be so angry that he won't even look at them. He'll just get on the phone to my dad and the police and I'll be in a police cell or on a boat to the west coast of nowhere before the end of the day.

The only way to sort this case is to get the evidence in front of so many people that it can't be ignored. And to do that I need the help of Carl Marks. Which is a problem.

I get to school about twenty minutes early and hang around outside the entrance waiting for Carl to turn up. I've never seen the school this early before. It feels different. There's only a few kids who've got the playground all to themselves. Teachers are parking their cars and chatting in the car park. It doesn't feel like my school. It's too quiet and too calm. I don't like it.

After about ten minutes it starts to fill up and I feel more comfortable. The more kids that get into the playground the more arguments break out. And the teachers coming in are driving faster and not stopping to chat any more. They run straight into school dragging these huge bags full of books which they probably take home every night but never mark.

'Hi, Mickey.'

I turn round. It's my first surprise of the day. And it's not a pleasant one. Katie Pierce and Julie Reece. This is the first time I've seen either of them get to school on time.

'Why are you hanging round the entrance, Mickey?'

'Are you trying to sell your body, Mickey?'

'Maybe some doctor will buy it for medical research, Mickey.'

I don't react. Yesterday they had me on the run but things have changed.

'How will you be voting in the election, Mickey?' Katie's determined to get a rise out of me. She likes to jump up and down on you when she thinks she's got you down.

'It would be a shame if Carl Marks didn't get one vote,' Julie points out.

'Wouldn't it?' agrees Katie. 'So you make sure, Mickey, that you put your little cross in the right little box. You can manage that, can't you?'

I can't walk off because I've got to wait for Carl so I look the other way.

'He's not saying anything, Katie.'

'He's not used to girls talking to him, Julie. Usually they just run off screaming when they see his face.'

Don't react, I tell myself. Don't give them the satisfaction.

'He's trying to pretend he's not bothered, Julie.'

'He's not doing a very good job of it, Katie.'

'If only he didn't always go so red.'

I can feel it happening. I try telling my

face to calm down but it isn't listening.

'Do you think he looks cute when he's blushing, Katie?'

'No, I think he looks uglier.'

'I didn't think that was possible.'

'I think when Tony gets to be Head Boy I'll get him to organize after school clubs for boys like Mickey so they can learn to wear bags over their heads to keep the rest of us from feeling sick every time we look at them.'

'Great idea, Katie. That will get him even more votes.'

I can't keep quiet any longer. There's only so much I can take. 'Let's wait for the result, Katie,' I tell her, 'before we start deciding what we're going to do.'

'He's talking,' says Julie.

'But he isn't making any sense,' Katie tells her.

There's no point trying to keep quiet now. I might as well try to find out something that's been nagging at me since the start of this case.

'All right,' I say. 'I admit it. You've probably won this one, Katie. But what's in it for you? Do you fancy Tony or something?'

Katie laughs. And she's got the kind of

laugh that makes you feel small no matter how many times you hear it.

'Oh, Mickey, you're so simple. You think everything has got to be connected with sex. Tony probably does fancy me – what boy in this school doesn't? – but I'm not in it for that.'

'Why then?'

'In two years' time, Mickey, I'm going to be in Year Eleven. And I'm going to be Head Girl. My mum wants me to be and I want to be. And I'm not having some stupid kids in Year Seven voting for some other girl and stopping me. As soon as Tony's been elected Head Boy he's going to see Mr Walton and tell him that the whole election process makes for bad feelings between pupils and that we'd be much better going back to the old system where he decided with the approval of my mum— all the governors.'

'Why does he need to be Head Boy to do that?' I ask her.

'Because, Mickey, and I'll say this very slowly so that you get it inside that little brain of yours, if the person who wins says the system is rubbish then Mr Walton has got to listen. But if Tony lost it might just sound as if he was moaning because he didn't win.

It's my destiny to be Head Girl of this school, Mickey, and I don't intend to allow a little thing like democracy to stop me. Close your mouth, Mickey.'

I do what she tells me. There are times when Katie Pierce blows my mind. I always think I know how bad she is and then I realize that I've hardly got a clue. She's managing this whole thing just so all the kids in the school can't stop her becoming Head Girl. In two years' time. Amazing.

She turns away. Then she checks back. 'One more thing, Mickey.'

I nod.

'I believe some casual smoking acquaintances of mine took it into their heads to advise you to stay away from the elections for Head Boy. Unfortunately, as your little tapeworm friend showed yesterday, you didn't take their advice. They were very angry when I told them, Mickey. I tried to counsel them to be calm but I don't know whether I succeeded. Watch your back, Mickey.'

She's already walking off with Julie and they're laughing.

This is seriously bad news. The Psychos are already after me and that's before they find out I've fingered them for bullying. And then something else hits me. I accused Nicola Cohen of setting The Psychos on me and she hadn't. It was Katie Pierce. I feel bad for a second but then I remember seeing her go into the strategy meeting yesterday. She must have known all about it.

I don't have much time to dwell on what The Psychos might do to me because I see Carl Marks walking into school. He looks just as insignificant as he did on the day I met him. Why did I ever take a case that involved turning such an obvious loser into a Head Boy? But I can think about that one when I'm in hospital recovering from whatever damage The Psychos do to me.

'Hey,' I shout to him. 'Wait a minute.'

He keeps walking. I catch him up.

'I need to talk to you.'

'Keep away from me,' he says. 'You've poisoned the democratic process. I could have been a contender and now I'm nothing but a bum.'

'You can still be a contender,' I say. 'You didn't have anything to do with what happened yesterday.'

'I have a conscience.'

'I've got a conscience too.'

'You don't know what a conscience is.'

Now that's a bit unfair. I may not be able to put it into words but I know what a conscience is. Vaguely.

'You've got to listen to me.'

'Take your hands off me.'

'One minute,' I tell him. 'Then you'll never have to speak to me again if you don't want to.'

'You can be sure of that,' he says but he doesn't go anywhere. At least I've got a chance. I've got to convince him to go back to being a politician. And to do that I've got to talk his language. Which is why for the first time this morning I stayed in the dining room with my dad to have my breakfast instead of eating it in front of the TV in the lounge. He listens to Radio 4, which has all these politicians telling lies about how great everything is. I've heard them. Now I've got to try and be them.

'Look around you, Carl,' I say.

He looks.

'What do you see?'

'Nothing unusual.'

'Keep looking.'

He turns all the way round. 'I don't see anything.'

'Don't you, Carl?'

'I'm getting out of here.'

He tries to shake me off but I keep hold of his arm.

'You gave me a minute, Carl. Let me tell you what I see.'

He looks angry. 'There isn't anything.'

'Look closer, Carl. Look over there at that kid with the ragged school uniform. Wouldn't he be happier in his own clothes? Look at that girl by the bike shed. She looks tired, Carl. Up all night doing homework. Wouldn't it be better if she only had to do thirty minutes a night? Look at that kid by the bin. He's probably got PE today and he'll be herded into a communal shower. Wouldn't it be better if he had an individual cubicle? Only you can do this, Carl. Only you can make these kids' lives better. They can't afford your conscience, Carl. They need you.'

I risk checking out how he's taking all this. It's my last throw of the dice and I'm finished if he doesn't buy it.

But he's bought it all right. He's got this kind of dreamy look on his face.

'Loathsome as you are, you've got a point,' he tells me. 'These kids need me. Perhaps I must sacrifice my moral scruples for the common good.'

I nod my head a lot to show him I'm agreeing.

'But,' he says.

I don't have much time. The last thing I want to hear is a 'but'.

'Yeah?' I try to sound casual.

'It's possible that I might not win,' he points out. 'I was distracted by you into putting too much energy into manoeuvring against the opposition when I should have been concentrating on getting my own message across. Still, perhaps if I do a really good speech at the final hustings I will convince enough people of the value of my case.'

That's the last thing I need. I've seen him speak before. If he does it again he'll probably lose the one vote he's going to get.

'Look, Carl,' I tell him. 'I know you would have won if it hadn't been for all these distractions.' He wouldn't have had a chance. 'And I know it's my fault that they happened but you've got to let me put it right. I can win you that election. All you've got to do is give me your five-minute slot and get a TV and a video on the stage. The one in the English department with the really big screen.'

'I don't know . . .' he says. 'You've made so many mistakes already.'

I'm really getting fed up with this. Without my help he'd be nowhere. But I can't afford to let him know.

'Carl, you've got to give me a chance to put things right. And remember it's not how you win. It's what you do after you win that matters. Remember these kids.'

'But how are you going to win it?'

The bell goes.

'There isn't enough time,' I tell him. 'Assembly starts in ten minutes. You've got to find that video player and get it set up.'

'But I—'

'It's now or never, Carl. What's it going to be?'

He stares into my face. I stare back. He nods.

'For the children,' he says.

And then he goes. It's a good thing. If I'd had to listen to any more garbage about 'the children' I'd have puked up.

But there's no time for vomiting – I'm back on the case.

CHAPTER 27

I've been telling myself I don't need the toilet for the past five minutes and it's just made me want it more. I've crossed my legs but that didn't work. I've tried to think of very dry things like deserts and camels and leaves. But my desert has an oasis in it, my camel's got humps full of water and the leaves end up being washed down a grid by a rainstorm.

I'm not going to go.

I'm sitting in the hall and Walton's about to start the assembly. About a minute ago Carl Marks and an English teacher brought in the big TV and VCR and got it up to the stage, which is good. What's not good is that I'm going to have to talk to the entire school and make sense if I'm going to bring this case home. Talking to the whole school. That must be about a thousand people. I've never spoken to more than about seven people at once in my life. What if I faint? What if my voice starts breaking up like it does sometimes? What if I wet myself?

I'm going to go.

'Sir,' I say to Mr Newman. I'm sitting right on the edge of the aisle so I can get out easily and I don't need to shout.

'What is it?' he says without looking at me.

'Can I go to the toilet?'

'Assembly is about to start.'

'I've got to go, sir.'

'Be quick then.'

I pull my coat on as I get up.

'You don't need your coat to go to the toilet.'

My coat's got the videos in and I'm not leaving them anywhere. 'Someone might nick it, sir.'

'Don't worry – I'll keep an eye on it.'

I put it on anyway. Newman doesn't look happy.

'*Quiet!*' It's Walton.

Newman looks at Walton. You can tell he doesn't want to be seen arguing with a kid in his class. 'Go on then.'

I slip into the aisle and head towards the back door. Behind me I can hear Walton starting the assembly. I slow down. If Carl Marks is going first then I'll have to risk wetting myself in front of a thousand people.

'*Today is the final hustings for the election of the Head Boy and Head Girl. Ladies come before gentlemen, as we all know, so we'll hear from the two candidates for Head Girl first and then from the two candidates for Head Boy. The candidates will speak in alphabetical order. After you've heard from all four you can go back to your tutor rooms and vote. We will announce the winners later in the day.*'

I get out of the hall. I've got about fifteen minutes before I need to speak. I wish I hadn't remembered about speaking to the whole school. It means I have to run to the toilets.

For once they're empty. Everybody is in assembly. Afterwards I go over to the mirror to check out how I look. If I'm going to stand up in front of a thousand people I want to look all right. I can't see any big spots, which is good, but my hair's gone a bit crazy, which isn't. I run some water into my hand and try and stick it down but it doesn't want to go. So I put some more on. Now it does stay down but it looks really greasy and horrible. So I shake my head to try and get some of the water off. I'm not normally this vain but then normally nobody looks at me. Finally I don't look too like I'm some mad scientist.

'Well, look who it is.'

I turn round. Standing in the doorway of the toilets are The Psychos.

They don't say anything more. They shut the door behind them and come towards me. I start moving backwards.

'Hi,' I say.

They still don't talk.

'How's it going?'

Nothing. I jolt to a stop as I hit the back wall.

'Do you want a fag?' I say. 'I'm gasping.'

I pull them out of my pocket and offer them around.

They don't even look at them. This is bad.

'You can have them all.'

I'm doing this all wrong. I sound desperate. The first rule of not getting beaten up is never sound desperate. Your only chance is to front them out. Look weak and they'll kill you. But it's not always that easy. Most kids, even ones with really hard reputations, won't do that much to you. Sometimes they'll be happy with seeing you lose face by running away or they'll just hit you a couple of times and that'll be it. Just enough to prove they're hard but not enough to do any real damage.

The Psychos are different. They are really dangerous. And they're all in my face.

And then the first fist goes into my stomach and I stop worrying and start surviving.

You hear all these kids who watch too many kung-fu movies with all the big talk about what they'd do if three kids tried to beat them up. How they'd hit the first one to come in the face, throw the second one over their back and drop kick the third one in the stomach. And then walk out of wherever it was whistling.

The real world isn't like that. When three kids decide to beat up one kid the three kids win. Always.

Because unlike the movies they don't come one at a time, they come all at once. One hits you, another shoves you and the last one kicks you. And then you go down.

All you can do then is roll yourself into a ball and try and keep the kicks away from the bits of you that matter like your head. You don't need to learn this – it just happens. And the kicks keep coming.

If you try and stand up then they knock you down again. So all I can do is try and work out who's going to kick me next and do my best to roll away. But it isn't that easy. With your head covered you can't see what's happening and with three people you get confused. So plenty of them manage to get through.

The strange thing is that after the first couple it doesn't hurt too much. I don't know why. It's like your body just forgets about normal things like pain and starts concentrating on trying to keep you alive. Which is good because if every one of the kicks was hurting as much as the first two I don't think I'd last that long.

And then the kicks stop. At first I think it's a good sign. But I'm wrong.

'We're not getting him.'

'What?'

'Pull him up.'

'What?'

'Grab his hair.'

That still hurts. My head goes up and a fist smashes straight into it. I feel blood running on my face.

'Get him up again.'

They might really kill me. And I don't know how to stop them. The hand grabs my head again and pulls it up.

'What do you think you're doing?'

The hand lets go of my head. I slump face down on the floor. I hear some shouting and some running. And then there's someone lifting me up. I look into Mr Newman's face.

'Are you OK, Mickey? Are you OK?'

I nod.

'We need to get you to the nurse.'

I don't have too much strength left but everything I've got goes into shaking my head.

CHAPTER 28

*'We come to the final candidate for Head Boy –
Carl Marks.'*

I don't like begging teachers but it was the
only way to get Newman to let me back into
the hall. I told him I felt OK and it was worse
than it looked. He's still fairly new and he
hasn't picked that many bleeding kids off
toilet floors. As soon as he said, 'I'm not sure
that's a good idea,' I knew I'd got him.

Which has got me back to the hall.
Whether I'm going to get on the stage is
another thing.

Carl Marks stands up. 'Hello,' he says and
then he pauses.

One thousand kids don't answer him.

'I'm not going to speak to you today.'

Some kid cheers.

'Oh,' he says and then he pauses again.
You can hear people coughing. He looks all
around him for a couple of seconds. It's like
he's forgotten why he's there. For a second I
see two of him. I focus really hard and there's

only one of him again. But that one is a bit blurry.

'Due to new information which has just come to light I am going to ask Mickey Sharp to speak to you. Thank you.'

I start walking before Newman has a chance to grab me. I'd only told him that I needed to give something to Carl Marks. I hadn't told him I was going to speak. And now is not the time to try and explain. Now's the time to put one foot in front of the other.

All the kids start turning round as I try to walk straight down the aisle. I keep my head down but I can still hear them.

'What's happened to his face?'

'Why's he got his coat on?'

'He's bleeding.'

'He's ugly.'

I don't look up until I get to the steps up to the stage. My head feels really numb and my legs are shaking. The steps aren't going to be easy. Still, there's only five of them and I get up the first three fine. It's only when I step towards the fourth and it begins to move that I hear a 'woo' from the hall and I realize that I've started swaying.

Come on, I tell myself. I've come this far. I'm not going to fall over now.

I stare as hard as I can at the steps and they become solid again. I get up the last two and I make it onto the stage.

'What's going on here?' says Walton coming nearer.

I look up. Thankfully there's only one of him. Two Waltons is more than I could cope with.

'I had a bit of an accident, sir,' I say, 'but I'm fine. Mr Newman's going to take me to the nurse in a couple of minutes. He said it was OK.'

'This is most irregular.' Tony Lejeune is right behind Walton. 'He can't speak to the school. He's not a candidate.'

'Mr Walton said we could use our five minutes however we want,' says Carl Marks, who's behind him. 'He said we could have a multimedia presentation.'

'He's not a multimedia presentation,' shouts Tony Lejeune.

'You said anything we like, didn't you, Mr Walton?'

'I didn't mean this,' Walton tells him.

'I didn't know that, sir. You've got to let him speak.'

'He's bleeding.'

'He's not bleeding that much.'

It's strange but while they're arguing I feel myself coming back to the world. Everything I'm looking at is getting brighter and stronger.

'I object,' says Tony.

'Sir,' says Carl Marks, 'you can't refuse my right to five minutes in front of the school. Think what message it would give the children about democracy.'

Walton looks at the hall. Tony, Carl and I look too. Everybody looks back. They all look confused. I can tell Walton doesn't know what to do. I don't figure he's too keen on letting me speak to the school but the whole election is going to be a disaster if he doesn't. After the Year Nine orchestra I don't think Walton wants any more disasters this week.

'Swear just once, Sharp, and you're expelled,' he says.

He heads back to his seat. Tony and Carl hit theirs. I'm standing on my own in front of the whole school. Things start swaying again.

'Hi,' I say. I can't believe it. I'm doing the same thing as Carl Marks and I get exactly the same response. There's nothing to do but keep going.

'I've got some new evidence about this Head Boy thing.'

'*Speak up!*' some kid yells out.

I don't know why but I try and spot him. There's no hope because you can't pick one face out of a thousand. I'm speaking to a thousand kids. The dizziness gets worse.

'Come on, Mickey,' I tell myself.

'*He's talking to himself!*' shouts out some girl.

'*He's mad!*' shouts out some boy.

And then the laughter comes. Lots and lots of laughter and it's all aimed at me. I've already been beaten up today and now I'm being laughed at by the entire school and it's not even half past nine. I look down. Then I look behind me. Carl Marks is looking at me desperately. Walton is beginning to get out of his chair and he's looking worried. But Tony Lejeune isn't even looking at me. He's just looking smug.

I think it's his smugness that makes me do it. He's so certain that he's going to win, so certain that Carl and me are just hopeless losers that I turn back to the whole school and yell, '*Quiet!*'

It works. The laughter stops. Before it can start again I shove my hand in my pocket and drag out a video and hold it in the air as high as I can.

'*I have here evidence which shows that Tony*

Lejeune and his team have cheated all the way through this campaign and must be disqualified.'

I jam the tape into the video and press play. As the picture of the Maths corridor comes up on the screen everybody shuts up.

'This is what happened to one of Carl Marks's posters stuck up in this school only two days ago.'

Everybody looks. It's a good thing all the English teachers are so big on showing videos that they spent all last year's budget on the biggest screen they could get. The picture is really sharp.

At first the Maths corridor is empty. Then Walton walks in. This is when I had to run off and wasn't able to see what happened next. There's a big 'Ooooh' from the kids in the hall when they see Walton. They'd love to see him get caught doing something wrong.

Walton strides down the corridor until he's right by Carl Marks's poster. He checks either side of him twice and then he does it. He picks his nose.

'Eeeeuuuurrrggghhh!'

One thousand kids make exactly the same noise. I don't blame them. I was nearly sick when I first saw it.

'Sharp,' threatens Walton.

The kids start laughing. But they stop

when Walton walks off because as soon as he's gone another person appears on the screen. This person walks straight up to the place where Carl Marks's poster is and rips it down.

There's a gasp from the kids in the hall.

'I can identify the person who tore that poster down,' I shout. *'That is Tony Lejeune's closest supporter, Katie Pierce.'*

There's a universal swivelling of heads as every kid in the hall turns round to look at her.

And then the best thing happens.

She starts going red.

'This is disgraceful.'

I turn round to find out that the person shouting behind me is not who I expected it to be. It's Tony Lejeune.

'Mr Walton, fellow pupils, I have been let down,' he shouts. *'The actions of Katie Pierce are a disgrace to the school. I condemn her without reservation. She is never to be trusted to hold high office.'*

I check Katie Pierce again. She's getting redder and redder.

'However,' Lejeune goes on, *'I had no idea she was behaving in this disgraceful way and I do not deserve to be punished because of it. You, the*

pupils of Hanford High, my friends, deserve the chance to vote for the Head Boy you want. I will not be beaten by this. I will fight on. I will rid the school of these foul practices. Vote for me, my friends.'

I can't believe it. Ten seconds ago Katie Pierce and him were best friends. Now he's the leader of the campaign against her.

'SILENCE!'

It's the biggest shout he's ever produced in all the time I've been in the school, which means that it nearly blows my eardrums apart. But it works. Walton gets the whole school quiet.

'Everybody listen. We've seen some very upsetting things on that tape but in this school we are innocent until proven guilty. If Tony can assure me that he had nothing to do with unfair election practices then I am prepared to let the election continue. Tony, can you give me that assurance?'

Lejeune lifts his head high in the air. Even to me he looks honest and decent and trustworthy, just a little sad at having been let down.

'I can, sir,' he says and his voice is strong and clear.

For a second I'm tempted to vote for him

myself. But instead I reach into the other pocket of my coat and pull out the second video.

Lejeune goes pale.

I jam it into the video and press play.

The kids at the front stand up to get a better view, which blocks the view of the kids behind them so they stand up too. Within a few seconds the whole school is standing up. Walton and the other teachers are too busy trying to get a good look themselves to tell them to sit down.

And what do they see?

They see Katie Pierce bribing Year Sevens with free dinner tickets. They see Kelvin Sleazer appear. They see the Year Sevens chanting, 'Tony! Tony!'

And watching it all and knowing that it is going on is Tony Lejeune.

I press stop as soon as Walton appears on the screen. The whole school stares at Tony Lejeune.

'*I can explain,*' he shouts.

The boos start.

'*It must be some kind of mistake,*' he yells.

The hisses follow.

'*People who meet me say I'm a straightforward guy,*' he screeches.

The whistles begin.

'*QUIET!*' yells Walton, who's looking very nervous. The school is beginning to get dangerous. Five minutes ago they couldn't care less about the Head Boy election but now they're ready to tear Tony Lejeune apart.

'*Due to this amazing new evidence,*' bellows Walton, '*I declare that Tony Lejeune is disqualified from the election.*'

Cheers and whoops from the school.

'*Therefore your new Head Boy must be—*'

He suddenly stops. He looks embarrassed. He's forgotten Carl's name. He turns round to ask Carl what it is, but in the moment of quiet some kid in the hall shouts,

'*MICKEY SHARP!*'

The school hear my name. I expect them to laugh. But they don't. The name spreads and they start chanting.

'*Mickey! Mickey! Mickey!*'

This is terrible. I don't want to be Head Boy.

'*NO!*' I shout, '*NO!*'

'*Mickey! Mickey! Mickey!*'

'*SHUT UP!*' I scream.

'*Mickey! Mickey! Mickey!*'

The school has gone completely crazy. Kids are jumping up and down.

'You meant to do this, didn't you?' Walton booms at me.

'No.'

'You've twisted the whole political process to benefit yourself, haven't you?' accuses Carl Marks.

'No.'

'I'll close this school down before I'll make you Head Boy,' Walton tells me.

'I don't want to be Head Boy,' I tell him.

But the kids aren't going to have it any other way. It's nothing to do with me any more, they've just gone mad. But they're going mad while chanting my name and I know the way the world works. I'll get the blame.

'Mickey! Mickey! Mickey!'

'They're out of control!' Miss Gartree shouts, coming up to Mr Walton. 'What are we going to do?'

'There's only one thing for it,' says Mr Walton.

He walks out through the nearest door but I can still see him through the window. He takes a quick look around him, lifts his fist and smashes the glass on a fire alarm.

'WAA-WAA-WAA.'

There are things you think you'll never see

and your Head Teacher setting off the fire alarm is one of them.

'*WAA-WAA-WAA.*'

The teachers start moving the kids out.

'*WAA-WAA-WAA.*'

'Can I have the first interview, mate?' Kelvin Sleazer is right beside me.

'Go away.'

'You're the school hero, mate. The school celebrity. You're going to be monster. You've got to talk to me, mate. Hey, Nicola. Get over here and talk this guy into giving us an interview.'

I look up when he says the name Nicola. But when I look at where he's talking I don't see Nicola Cohen anywhere. All I see is Katie Pierce's friend, Julie Reece. She looks at Kelvin Sleazer and then she looks at me.

'Nicola, get over here, mate.'

Julie starts moving away fast.

'Nicola? What's the matter?' Sleazer shouts after her.

And then the thing which has been banging around inside my head since last night crashes into place. When Nicola Cohen dumped her books on my table I noticed how neat her handwriting was. And I'd seen that handwriting somewhere before but I couldn't remember where. But now I can. On the letter that Katie Pierce had dropped on my desk by mistake when she was having a gloat over my sister being a prize in the school paper. A letter written by Nicola Cohen and addressed to Kelvin Sleazer. I know about only one letter that Nicola wrote to him. The letter which told Kelvin Sleazer that Nicola had resigned. Which Katie Pierce somehow got hold of. What if she got hold of it before Kelvin Sleazer ever saw it? That means Kelvin Sleazer wouldn't have known she'd resigned but Katie Pierce would have done. Which means that Katie Pierce could have got someone to pretend to be Nicola Cohen and write all those pro-Lejeune articles. Which might explain why Kelvin Sleazer has just called Julie Reece 'Nicola'. That means—

'Mickey! Get outside now. There's a fire,' shouts Mr Newman.

My brain can't take any more. The dizziness starts coming back. I see two Mr Newmans, three Kelvin Sleazers. The hall starts spinning, the fire alarm's shriek feels like it's inside me.

And then everything goes dark.

CHAPTER 29

'I'm going to kill you.'

It's the third time she's said it and I'm not dead yet so I figure that I'm safe. I carry on reading the newspaper.

NEW HEAD BOY MAKES MARKS

Hanford High's new Head Boy Carl Marks emerged from a meeting with Mr Walton claiming that 'things could only get better for the pupils of Hanford High'. He explained that for reasons of cost he had agreed with Mr Walton that the school could not have individual shower cubicles and that for reasons to do with the timetable pupils couldn't pick their own teachers. He further agreed with Mr Walton that parents wouldn't like it if their children were only allowed to do half an hour's homework a night. However, Marks insisted that he had won a significant battle on school uniform. Whilst still having to wear it, pupils will now be allowed to wear earrings which dangle down one and a half centimetres rather than the previous one centimetre. 'This is a great victory for the pupils,' Marks announced. He added that he had appointed a Uniform Tsar to tell everybody of their new rights. The position has gone to a controversial new face in the Marks team – Katie Pierce. Marks laughed off suggestions that Katie Pierce had been discredited and humiliated last week during the dramatic hustings which had seen his unopposed election. 'All that is in the past,' he said. 'Katie is a talented individual who has the best interests of the school at heart.' He also announced that there would be no more elections for the position of Head Boy and Head Girl. 'After the disgraceful scenes of last week,' Marks explained, 'when a small minority of pupils stole a fire engine following the chaos of the election, it was felt that Hanford High just isn't ready for democracy.' So far the school has not managed to find the miscreant who set the fire alarm off though Marks insisted that Mr Walton was giving the matter his highest priority.

by Nicola Cohen

I suppose I should have expected it. Carl Marks hasn't spoken to me in the week since last Friday. He paid me all right but the money was pushed under the door of my shed when I wasn't there and when I see him about the school he looks the other way. At first I thought it was because there'd been all the chants for me to be Head Boy even though that didn't last long. After the fire alarm everyone went back to class and Walton sent a kid round saying that I couldn't be Head Boy because I wasn't in Year Eleven. It had to be Carl Marks as he was the only candidate left. Which was fine with me because I never wanted to be Head Boy. But from the sound of the newspaper story there's plenty of reasons why Carl's ignoring me. Now he's friends with Katie Pierce and all future elections have been called off. She'll probably make Head Girl in the end.

I haven't seen Walton either, which surprises me. I expected to be in his office first thing Monday morning trying to explain the theft of the school security videos but I haven't heard a thing. Mr Newman kept me back after registration and told me that The Psychos were being expelled for their assault

on me and that Mr Walton felt that the bullying I had been suffering had affected my
mind and had decided to take no further
action. So my parents never got to hear about
it and so I don't have to go and live with
goats on the west coast of nowhere.

So I suppose I should be happy.

'I'm going to kill you.'

Which brings me to the problem of my
sister.

I couldn't stand the thought of my sister
having a date with one of the morons at the
back. So I did a deal with Kelvin Sleazer. In
return for my exclusive interview on how I
solved the Head Boy case he had to do me
two favours – the first one was to make sure
that I won the date competition. Which is
how I end up sitting at a candle-lit table for
two in the middle of the canteen with my
sister. They've put candles on it even though
it's lunch time to make it special. It's not
working.

'You've ruined my life,' hisses Karen.
'Everybody's laughing at me.'

I don't think it's the surprise date she was
hoping for.

'I'm never going to do anything for Kelvin
Sleazer again in my life. He said he was

going to make me a star in this school and instead he's made me a fool.'

'They only build you up to knock you down, Karen,' I tell her.

'You're going to pay for this Mickey,' she tells me. 'I'm going to talk to Mum about your diet. I can make sure you never eat anything but salad again. So eat up that burger because it might be your last.'

I'm about to do what she says. I'm trying to con her into thinking I'm not bothered about sitting here but it's not true. Going on a date with your sister does nobody's image any favours.

'Can I have your autograph, please?'

I turn round. Behind me is a Year Seven kid. It's really embarrassing. Ever since last Friday they think I'm some kind of hero and about ten have asked me for my autograph already. I started off saying no because I thought they were laughing at me but this kid looks OK.

'What's your name?'

'Terence.'

He gives me his homework diary and I sign it.

'I don't believe this,' Karen shouts at him. 'What are you asking for his autograph for?

He's my little brother. If you want someone's autograph you should ask for mine. I'm the person who's going to be a star round here.

Terence takes one look at her, grabs his homework diary back and runs.

'I'm sick of this,' says Karen. 'I'm going.'

She stands up and stalks off, trying to walk like a model, but she bangs into the pile of assorted baguettes by the door so it doesn't quite come off.

I'm left all alone at my romantic dinner table. I think it might be time to get out of here before I end up looking even more of an idiot.

Which is when I see her.

She's leaning against the Coke machine with her notebook in her hand.

'Nicola,' I shout without thinking where I am.

The whole canteen goes quiet.

'Come over here,' I say, trying to pretend I haven't noticed that everybody else is listening.

She looks like she's not sure, but with everybody looking at her I figure she can't think of anything else to do. So she walks over and sits down opposite me. I can see the candles reflected in her eyes. She looks good.

The rest of the canteen rapidly lose interest. They were hoping for an argument and we've let them down.

'Haven't seen you around much,' I say.

'I've been busy.'

'I know. I read your thing. It's good.'

'Thank you.'

There's a silence. I remember the smile she gave me when she was telling me that she'd conned Walton and Gartree over the toilet thing. No other girl has ever smiled at me like that.

'If that's all, I'll be going,' she says.

'No,' I say.

'What do you want then?'

I try to answer her question but when I open my mouth something else comes out.

'I got your job back like I promised.'

That was the other favour I got off Kelvin Sleazer.

'And I got Kelvin Sleazer to recommend to Walton that you're the next editor.'

She doesn't say anything.

'So, we both came out of this OK, right?'

She still doesn't say anything. It's not much of a conversation when there's only one person talking.

'I found out that Katie Pierce took your

resignation letter off Sleazer's desk before he saw it. She dropped it in front of me by accident a couple of days ago but I didn't figure out what it was then. Sleazer had never met you so Katie got Julie Reece to pretend to be you and change the poll and then write more pro-Lejeune stories. She never let Sleazer see Julie with the rest of the Lejeune team so that even if Julie got found out they could deny any knowledge of her. That's why Katie sent Julie away before Sleazer came to cover the dinner tickets story. It worked because Sleazer had never seen you before. And I checked your timetable. You did have Maths in that room last lesson that day. You had nothing to do with the strategy meeting.'

'I knew all that,' she tells me.

'Oh, right.'

'I knew all that the night I came to see you in your shed but you wouldn't listen to me. I'd also found out that the school hasn't got enough money to pay for individual shower cubicles which is why Walton and Gartree weren't exactly in favour of Carl Marks at the hustings – even though they had nothing to do with rigging the election. But you didn't want to know about that. You just wanted to shout and yell at me.'

'Things were a bit confused,' I tell her. 'I made a mistake.'

'I know that too.'

'I'm sorry,' I tell her. 'Can I make it up to you? I figured we could maybe ... you know ...'

'No, I don't.'

'We could maybe see a movie sometime or go for a walk or – I don't know – what do you like? Newspapers, right? Maybe we could go and buy a newspaper together or something.'

'You're asking me out.'

It's not candles sparking her eyes now. The whole canteen goes quiet again. They're going to get their argument after all.

'Last week you were calling me a liar and a cheat and a two-faced traitor and now you want to go out with me.'

It doesn't sound too good when she puts it like that.

'I go out with boys who trust me, Mickey. Not paranoid creeps who think I'm a liar.'

'It was the case,' I say quietly. 'I got too caught up in trying to solve it.'

'Don't blame the case for what's going on inside you.'

She's standing up as she says this. When

she's finished she turns round and walks across the canteen. She's the second girl to walk out on me in five minutes. But Nicola avoids the pile of assorted baguettes, which makes her exit all the more impressive and makes me feel an even bigger fool.

She pushes open the door to the playground and disappears through it. A gust of cold wind rushes through the opened door. The candles on my table struggle for a second and then go out.

THE END